MW01195875

CYNTHIA HICKEY

Cowboy Pitfall

Cynthia Hickey

The Cowboys of Misty Hollow

ISBN-13: 978-1-965352-31-1

Chapter One

Isabella Harper parked in front of the Willow Ridge Inn. Guilt poured over her that it had taken her grandmother's death to bring her back to the house that had been filled with so much love when Bella was a child.

Now, the house belonged to her, along with her grandmother's wish that Bella keep the bed-and-breakfast up and running. Now, here she was, having given her resignation as sous-chef in the restaurant she'd once wanted to be head chef in. Scary how one letter could turn her life plans upside down.

She opened her car door and stepped onto the pea gravel that made up the inn's circular drive. Built on five acres and surrounded by magnolia, oak, and willow trees, the inn was close enough to the town of Misty Hollow to be convenient and still evoke the feeling of isolation.

She loved the old Victorian with gingerbread trim and turrets. Already her mind registered the fact the house was sadly in need of some exterior repairs—painting mostly, landscaping, and a new coat of stain on the front porch floor.

Pulling the key from the pocket of her denim capris, she headed for the front door. "Come on, Ghost." Her husky mix jumped over the back seat and out the driver side door. "Stay close, buddy. Don't wander off. This is new territory for you."

The nicker of a horse sent her heart into her throat. To her left, where the original brick house that had to be two-hundred years old stood, a black horse with a white blaze stuck its head over the fence. When had her grandmother gotten a horse and why had no one told her? Bella had no idea how to care for a horse.

Had someone been feeding the poor thing in the week since her grandmother passed? Bella put that task at the top of her to-do list.

The key inserted into the lock easily. The double doors squeaked as Bella pushed them open. One more thing to fix. She pulled her phone from her back pocket and started making a list. It might be a while before the inn could reopen at this rate.

She breathed deep of the spring air that followed her into the house, blowing away the musty odor of a house closed up. A sweeping staircase led to the second floor. To her right was the front room, or parlor as Grandmother liked to call it. Off that would be Grandma's office. To Bella's right was the large dining room that led to the kitchen.

Bella climbed the stairs, brushing her hand over the carved banister in need of polishing. At the top, she peered into her grandmother's bedroom, surprised to see that the bedrooms had been updated while still keeping their old country charm. Same with the bathrooms. Her grandmother's room would now be hers, leaving the other five to one day be rented out.

Thankfully, she'd inherited enough money to live off of and do the needed repairs until the inn once again made a profit. She glanced out the bedroom window. Ghost and the horse touched noses. Bella smiled. Her dog had found a friend.

After a quick walk-through of the house, jotting notes into her phone, Bella headed for the kitchen. "Oh, how nice." Grandma had updated the appliances. The cupboards needed to be sanded and repainted, but at least the main items were done. All this work just before she died. Had she had a premonition?

Bella perched on a stool at the kitchen island and watched Ghost and the horse frolic in the pasture. The doctor who'd called her a week ago said her grandmother had died of a heart attack. How was that possible when just days before her primary doctor had said Grandma's heart was still strong at the age of seventy-two?

She shook her head. The world would not be the same without the feisty old woman with a heart as big as Arkansas. Again, guilt over not having returned to the inn in over five years assailed Bella. She'd kept up the weekly phone calls, but had that been enough for her grandmother? During their last conversation, Grandma had seemed distracted. Mentioned someone wanting to buy the inn, but she had no intentions of selling what had been in the family for generations. Had the stress of someone wanting to purchase her home caused her heart attack?

Bella jumped off the stool.

The back door opened and a tall, dark-haired man wearing a black cowboy hat strode in.

Bella jumped back and screamed.

Ghost barked and burst into the kitchen behind the stranger.

The man whipped around toward Ghost.

~

"Whoa, boy." Deacon held up his hands in a protective gesture. "Call off your dog, ma'am." He glanced back at the tiny, blond woman with big eyes the color of a summer sky. Miss Harper's granddaughter most likely. He'd been expecting her.

"Who are you?"

"Deacon Simpson. You must be Isabella Harper. I help your grandmother around here when I can. Are you going to call off your dog?"

"Ghost, it's okay. Yes, I'm Isabella Harper. People call me Bella." She narrowed her eyes. "Grandma never told me she had a handyman."

Deacon lowered his hands and set his hat on the island. "I'm not a regular. Work when I can. Mostly making sure Blaze out there is taken care of."

She climbed onto the bar stool. "I wasn't aware Grandma had a horse."

"He's a rescue. She got him a couple of weeks ago." He crossed his arms, then seeing how that might come across as negative body language, uncrossed them. "What are your intentions?"

"Regarding the inn? I plan on keeping it going, doing some repairs...which is what Grandma wanted." She tilted her head. "How did she seem to you in the days before she died? Are you the one who found her?"

He swallowed past the boulder rising in his throat. "Yes. I found her by the front door when I came in to tell her I'd finished exercising Blaze. She seemed fine.

A little worked up over a real estate developer coming around too many times wanting to buy." He chuckled. "She ran him off at gunpoint once. That was a sight." He'd fallen in love with the older woman from the first time he'd met her at Lucy's diner and overheard her asking for a part-time handyman. Since he wanted to save money to purchase land of his own someday, he'd offered his services. "She hadn't acted ill or anything. Seemed in perfect health. Why are you asking?"

She exhaled a heavy breath. "It's bothering me. I have a strong feeling something isn't right, and it's not only that I miss her."

He'd had the same thought but had kept his suspicions to himself. "The autopsy showed a heart attack."

"There are ways to make it look like one."

He stiffened. "Are you saying you suspect murder?"

She shrugged. "I don't know what I'm saying...yet. But, I intend to do some digging."

"If your suspicions are correct, that could be dangerous." Although he doubted anyone would take the petite "Barbie" doll of a woman seriously.

"I'm not scared." She hopped off the stool. "Introduce me to my horse."

"Do you ride?" He grabbed his hat.

"It's been a while, but I'm sure it's like riding a bike. I've never taken care of a horse, though."

He noticed she had to run to keep up with him and slowed his pace. "Do you plan on keeping me on? Keep in mind, I'm only here for a couple of hours each evening and one day on the weekend."

"Yes. I'll take what I can get, thank you. It'll make

the work go faster. I'll have a list of what needs done posted on the refrigerator by morning. If you could unload the trunk of my car before you head home, I'd appreciate it. I've got a U-Haul arriving in the morning."

His head started to hurt with all the talking. Sure, he'd share a daily cup of coffee with Mrs. Harper, but most of the time, they'd simply sat on the back deck and watched the birds feed.

He led Bella into the old house now used as a barn and storage room and showed her where everything she'd need for Blaze was kept. Then, he showed her where the tools were stored in case she wanted to get started on some of the repairs herself.

The Willow Ridge Inn had once run at full capacity. Then, Mrs. Harper had sent everyone away using the excuse of renovating. Sure, she'd made improvements, but Deacon suspected she'd stop renting rooms for another reason—one that left him with a bad feeling in his gut. A reason he intended to find out.

His gaze landed on Bella. The pretty little gal seemed as full of spark as her grandmother. Maybe with the two of them searching, they might find out what really happened here. If…her grandmother's death had indeed been something more than a heart attack.

Leaving Bella to get acquainted with Blaze, he headed for her car and popped the trunk. It didn't take long to cart the two suitcases, massive dog bed, and food and water dishes into the house. He left the dishes in the kitchen, then carried the rest to Mrs. Harper's bedroom—Bella's room now.

He stood there and studied the new striped wallpaper. A colorful quilt lay folded at the foot of the four-poster bed. An armoire stood opposite the window. Most of these old houses had secret tunnels dug during the prohibition years, but he had yet to find one in this house.

If his old friend had died suspiciously, there could be secrets hidden somewhere in these walls. Secrets that would answer a lot of questions.

"What are you doing?"

He jerked at Bella's sharp tone. "Carrying in your suitcases."

"You look as if you were searching for something." She arched a brow. "Mind telling me what?"

"Fine. I agree with you. Your grandmother's death may be more than we think." He pulled his cell phone from his pocket and pulled up a photo he'd taken when he'd found her dead. "It looks like she might've tried scratching something in the wood of the floor."

Bella squinted. "I don't see it."

"Come on." He led her downstairs and pointed. "Could that be an HD?"

She scratched her head. "Could be, but it's so faint. It might not be anything."

"Or it could be everything."

Chapter Two

The next morning, Bella tried opening the rolltop desk in her grandmother's "office." Nothing more than a place to pay bills and write letters. Yes, she still wrote letters by hand, or had.

The rolltop stuck halfway up. Bella leaned over and peered inside, then reached up to dislodge whatever prevented the desk from opening. Her fingers brushed against a thin book of some kind. With a grunt, she stretched farther and pulled the item free. The desk opened easily afterwards.

Bella stared at a thin, leather journal full of handwritten notes. What a treasure she'd found. Her grandmother's private thoughts. She sat in the office chair and started reading. Most of the entries were simply to-do lists and reminders, but the more she read, the more notes were written in the margins. "*He's watching*" and "*I know what he wants. He can't have it.*"

Bella frowned. Who could her grandmother be writing about? The man wanting to purchase the inn? Then why not state his name?

"So many questions, Ghost." She set the journal in

the top desk drawer and returned to unpacking the items that would go into what was now her office. Books, a printer, a laptop, none of which fit on the old-fashioned desk. She'd need to purchase something more suited to her needs when she went into town for groceries.

"Watch the house, boy." She patted her dog's head and grabbed her phone and car keys. Hopefully, she wouldn't have to drive to Langley to find a desk. If so, she'd order one online.

The mercantile didn't have what she needed, so online it would be. Next stop, groceries.

At first, she thought the sideways glances, then the ducking of heads were figments of her imagination, but when the whispers started, she realized the folks of Misty Hollow were looking at her with suspicion. She filled her cart as fast as possible, then rushed to the checkout line.

A woman behind her tapped her on the shoulder. "You're Mildred Harper's granddaughter, aren't you?"

"Yes, ma'am." Bella smiled.

"Be careful," the woman whispered. "Don't go nosing around. Some things are better left buried."

"What does that mean? Are you referring to the inn? I'm not selling."

A flicker of approval appeared in the woman's eyes before she moved to another line.

"Not everyone liked your grandmother, you know. No offense," the cashier said as she rang up Bella's items. "She wasn't exactly popular toward the end of her life. Shutting down the inn the way she did kept away the tourists, some say."

"What?" How could someone say something so mean? And Bella definitely took offense. Her smile faded.

The cashier shrugged. "People talk. Some say Mildred acted strange…paranoid. There were rumors that she might be losing her mind. She started staying to herself except for that cowboy she hired."

Bella needed to ask Deacon some more questions. Maybe the handyman wasn't as good as he seemed.

A man approached her as she loaded the groceries into the trunk of her car. "Mildred's death was unfortunate. People don't really like to talk about it."

"Why not?" Bella closed the trunk and faced him. "What are people not telling me?"

"Some say she didn't die of natural causes. Say she had enemies…knew something she shouldn't. You might not want to go digging, ma'am. This town…has a way of keeping its secrets."

"What makes people think I'm going to dig around?" She planted fists on her hips. Her heart pounded.

"Rumors, is all. Be careful, Miss Harper." He climbed into a beat-up truck parked next to her and drove off.

She watched until he disappeared around the corner, then climbed into her car before someone else approached with more cryptic messages and warnings. This morning had confirmed her fear that her grandmother hadn't died of natural causes. Proving it would be difficult, though, considering her death had been ruled a heart attack.

When she returned home, Ghost scurried to meet her. His jumping and spinning in circles never failed to make her smile. "Too bad you can't help me carry in these groceries." She popped the trunk and loaded as many bags as she could carry in her arms.

Three trips later, she started putting things away while she decided what task to tackle that day. What she really wanted to do was spend more time in her grandmother's journal. There had to be answers there. Maybe even an explanation of the HD scratched into the floor, if that's really what the marking was.

After retrieving the journal from the desk, she made herself a cup of coffee and settled down at the kitchen island. One entry toward the end of the journal froze the hand holding the mug halfway to her lips. *I got a letter today. One that said I've been asking too many questions and to stop if I didn't want to end up like the others. What others? What is it this person thinks I know*?

From what she'd written, her grandmother had no idea why someone was harassing her.

"Good morning."

Bella shrieked and dropped the mug, spewing coffee as the mug shattered against the tile floor.

~

Bella glared his way. "Don't sneak up on people like that!"

Deacon grinned. "Didn't mean to. I thought you would've heard the screen door."

"I didn't." She closed the journal.

"You found Mildred's journal. She was always writing in that thing." He motioned his head toward the coffeepot. "Do you mind?"

"Go ahead while I clean this up." She grabbed a handful of paper towels, then knelt on the floor.

"I'll get that." He picked up the broken pieces of

her mug. "Anything interesting in the journal?"

Suspicion flickered in her eyes. "Why?"

"No reason." What was wrong with her? The friendly woman from yesterday had disappeared.

She tossed the soaked paper towels in the garbage, leaned against the counter, and crossed her arms. "Folks in town were saying some interesting things today."

"Like what?" He poured a cup of coffee, preferring it black, and wondered why her trip to town concerned him.

"Lots of speculation about my grandmother staying to herself except for you. That she might've been asking questions she shouldn't have." Her gaze flicked to the journal.

"The part about her sticking to herself is true, at least the last few days of her life." He took a sip of his coffee. When Bella's eyes narrowed, he set the cup down. "I could tell something was bothering her, but she ignored my questions. Pretty much the same as you are. What kind of speculations, Bella? Because if they're about me, I can assure you I was very fond of Mildred and would never harm her."

"People seem to feel the same as I do. That my grandmother was murdered." She glanced at the journal again as if she were considering whether or not to fill him in on what it contained. Having decided, she took a deep breath. "There are several notations in the journal that back up what those people were saying. Grandma never mentioned a name, but she wrote about being watched and someone thinking she knew stuff she didn't."

He stared without speaking for several minutes. Why hadn't Mildred ever said anything to him? "I wish

I would've known. Maybe I could've helped her." She'd had many opportunities when they'd watched the sun set over the mountain in the evenings.

"Grandma wasn't one to involve others in her problems." Bella's shoulders slumped. "I need to find out who killed her, but I have no idea where to start."

"No, you need to let the sheriff know. If your suspicions are correct, this is dangerous. Someone has already committed murder to keep something quiet."

"I'll go to the sheriff, but I won't sit back and do nothing. If my grandmother was murdered, then justice needs to be done." She marched from the kitchen, grabbing the journal on her way.

Deacon followed. "Where are you going?"

"To the sheriff." She narrowed her eyes. "Didn't you just say I should?"

"Yes, but I didn't think you would so abruptly. I'll drive."

"Come on, Ghost." The dog raced for the front door.

Ten minutes later, leaving the dog in the truck, the receptionist ushered them into the sheriff's office. Deacon was surprised to see Sheriff Westbrook still there. "I thought you retired."

"New sheriff needs a few more days. Couple of weeks maybe." His chair squeaked under his weight. "What can I do for you, Miss Harper?"

Bella told him about what the people in town had said and what she'd read in her grandmother's journal. The sheriff's gaze remained locked on her while she spoke. When she finished, he folded his hands on the desk and leaned forward. "The autopsy showed a heart attack."

"Yes, but there are ways to make things look like a heart attack, aren't there?" She tilted her head. "Some plants and medicines?"

"You watch too many crime shows, ma'am."

She slapped the journal on the desk. "Please read this for yourself. I'm sure you'll come to the same conclusion. Will you?"

The sheriff nodded. "If I do come to believe your grandmother was murdered, I promise to do everything I can to achieve justice for her and you. If a murder was committed, do not try to solve this on your own, Miss Harper."

"I've already told her that," Deacon said. "I get the impression Bella does as she wants."

"I'll return the journal when I've finished." The sheriff slid the book into a desk drawer. "Anything else?"

Bella stood and shook her head. "No. Thank you for your time."

Outside, she faced Deacon. "He isn't going to help."

"Yes, he will. You heard him. Sheriff Westbrook is the best." He put his hand on the small of her back, enjoying the feel of her warmth through the shirt she wore. "How about grabbing something to eat at the diner? Ghost will get a free burger. It'll also give you a chance to meet some more of the townsfolk."

"I got the impression they were angry at my grandmother for temporarily shutting down the inn. Something about tourists." Since she didn't say no to supper, he let the dog out of the truck and headed for the diner.

"Spring is tourist season, but there are other places

for people to stay."

"I'm only repeating what was said."

He opened the diner door for her while she ordered Ghost to stay. Inside, the hostess led them to a booth near the window and handed them menus.

Several heads turned their way, then turned back to their meals. Not so strange. Newcomers were always scrutinized. Once Bella was accepted, the residents of Misty Hollow would have her back if trouble came.

When trouble came. He had no doubt now that Mildred had been murdered. Deacon would do everything in his power to find out why and to keep her granddaughter from suffering the same fate.

Chapter Three

Ghost's barking pulled Bella away from painting trim in the foyer. She set down the brush and stepped onto the porch as a man in a tailored navy suit exited a charcoal-gray Mercedes.

The man exuded confidence as he strode toward her, a dentist-whitened smile on a spray-tanned face set her off right away. The man's friendly demeanor seemed as fake as a three-dollar bill. His expensive cologne reached Bella before he did. She knew his kind. He was here to present her with a proposition and felt sure she'd accept.

"Welcome to Willow Ridge Inn. I'm sorry to say we aren't taking guests at this time." She pasted on a smile.

"Oh, I'm not here for a room, Miss Harper. Name is Garrett Boyd." His bright smile widened. "I'm here to offer you a deal."

Just as she thought. "If you're here to try and purchase the inn, I'm not interested."

"Neither was your grandmother, but I thought you'd listen to reason." He propped one shiny-shoe-covered foot on the bottom step. "The inn is lovely. A gem of Misty Hollow's history, but why would a young woman like yourself want to be burdened with such a place? You must know this prime piece of real estate could be something much grander. You'd walk away a rich woman and could do anything you want."

"I am doing what I want, Mr. Boyd." She crossed her arms.

"Picture something grand." He waved his arms as if envisioning a different landscape, most likely the demolition of the inn and a grand resort in its place—at least his definition of grand. More like a blight in the town of Misty Hollow.

"I can see you need more convincing." He held up a finger, then retrieved a briefcase from his car. "I've been putting together a plan for a luxury resort the likes this town has never seen." He pulled out a laminate sketch.

Bella glanced at the drawing of modern, glass-fronted buildings, a large, manicured lawn, a swimming pool and spa, all set against the backdrop of her beloved woods.

"This could be the jewel of the region. Tourists would flock here creating more jobs."

"We already have tourists. People who return time and time again to stay in this inn." A pool might not be a bad idea, though. This glass monstrosity was everything the inn wasn't. Cold instead of warm. Stark instead of welcoming.

Boyd leaned in a bit, dropping his voice as if sharing a secret between friends. "I know the idea is difficult." A flash of empathy flickered across his face, at least what he thought was empathy. "Your grandmother, bless her heart, did her best, but this place is a lot for one woman, isn't it? Running it by yourself." His gaze scanned the surrounding area. "Nostalgia isn't enough to survive, Miss Harper. It takes money, investment, modernization…management that can take it to the next level."

"I am the new management." A knot formed in her stomach. Had he implied she wasn't capable of running the Willow Ridge Inn?

His forced charm now seemed like a weapon, blurring the line between advice and insult. Arrogance shone in his eyes. He actually believed she'd cave. When she didn't respond, Boyd's smile faltered. "Look. I'm offering you a way out. Like I said, the amount I'm willing to pay will make you a very rich woman."

After a few uncomfortable moments of silence, he shook his head, sliding the sketch back into his briefcase. "Let's be honest." His words dripped with condemnation. "The tourism market is growing. The big resorts are drowning the small places like yours. Once my project is up and running, competition is going to be fierce. It'd be a shame to watch the Willow Ridge fade away because you're too stubborn to sell now for a good price." His chilly gaze locked with hers. "If you don't sell, I'll simply find someone else who will. Then, I'll shut you down out of sheer competition. You cannot win against me, Miss Harper."

She suppressed the urge to shudder. "Do not threaten me, Mr. Boyd. This town will stand beside me against investors like you."

His eyes narrowed. "I respect your decision, but understand that things can change. Opportunities like this don't come often. I'm sure you'll see things my way sooner or later. Be careful, Miss Harper. A young woman, alone as you are…well, things can happen."

~

Deacon stepped around the corner of the house in time to hear the man's last words. "She isn't alone, sir."

The man's eyes widened.

"Deacon, this is Garrett Boyd. He offered to buy the inn," Bella said. "I refused."

"Then Mr. Boyd should be on his way, shouldn't he?" Deacon refused the hand the man started to offer.

"Have it your way. I'll be seeing you around, Miss Harper." The man marched back to his car and sped away.

"You okay?" Deacon faced Bella.

"He threatened me." She sat on a wicker chair on the porch. "He basically said he'd force me out by building something better than the Willow Ridge Inn."

"Folks around here prefer the quaintness of this place. Sure, some will flock to town because of a resort, but I guarantee this inn will still remain at full capacity. You offer a personal touch that people will want." He didn't like the man threatening her. "I've got some vacation time coming to me, so I'll be around more."

"You don't have to spend your time off working here."

"This doesn't seem like work to me." He grinned. "I enjoy construction."

She looked skeptical. "If you say so. I am going to add some amenities to the inn, though. A pool, horseback riding, hikes…things that will draw people in. Maybe even offer long-term rentals. If we renovate the attic into suites…" She stepped off the porch and stared at the roof. "Yes, I think that will work."

Deacon's job list grew by a bunch. "I'll see to

anything you want doing, but some of that will require me to hire experts."

"Grandma left enough funds. I'll draw up a list of ideas, and we can go over them. You know this town better than I do." She climbed the stairs and entered the house.

Deacon needed to find out all he could about Garrett Boyd. He sent a quick text to his buddy, Deputy Hudson, who sent a quick reply that he'd run the man through the system and get back to him. Having done all he could for the moment, Deacon returned to the barn. If Bella planned on giving horseback rides, she'd need more horses, thus sturdy stables to put them in and full-time help to care for them.

She was also going to need to hire help, whether she realized it or not. One woman could not do it all. He'd check with Mrs. White, the Rocking W's cook, for her recommendations. While he worked, Deacon made a mental list of his own to go over with Bella.

"Stay for supper?" Bella interrupted his thoughts as she entered the barn. "I made spaghetti and garlic bread."

"Sounds good. I'll be in after I clean up." He headed for the spigot on the side of the barn.

"You can clean up in the house, you know." She laughed and left him to wash his hands and face with the soap and rag he kept on a hook near the spigot. Yes, he could use the house, but since he always removed his shirt to wash the grime from his face and neck, he hadn't wanted to offend Mrs. Harper. He wasn't sure how Bella would react. It was better to keep doing things the same way he always had.

The aroma of hot garlic bread greeted him when he

entered the kitchen. A bowl of spaghetti sat on the table next to a smaller bowl of grated parmesan cheese. His stomach rumbled, reminding him how long ago lunch time had been.

"There's tea in the fridge, if you'll pour us some." Bella carried a salad to the table. "I'm going to start cooking things I'll serve to guests, so I need a guinea pig to test the food on."

"I'm definitely happy to oblige." He grinned and poured two glasses of tea, then carried them to the table. "Have you thought about hiring help when you open?"

"Why?" She frowned.

"You can't care for the guests, cook, and clean all yourself." He heaped spaghetti onto his plate. "Plus, you'll need a gardener and someone to care for the horses."

"Oh." She plopped into her chair. "I guess that's too much for you to do in your off time."

"Yep." He grabbed two slices of bread. "I've also asked my friend with the sheriff's office to look into Garrett Boyd."

"Thank you." She pushed a notepad over to him. "These are some of my ideas for the inn."

He scanned the list. "You want to hold weddings and receptions here?"

"And parties. We can fix up the old barn. I know the horse is kept in the rock house, but the old barn just needs minor repairs. The property is pretty enough for wedding receptions." She tilted her head. "I'd get more use out of that than a pool. An event venue can be available for use all year."

"Mmm." This was going to take time and money.

"I think you should start renting out some rooms. You're going to need the funds."

"Sure. I've listed things in the order I'd like them done. The event venue is first." She sprinkled cheese over her pasta. "While that's in the works, we can look into purchasing some horses. Five should be enough, right?" She rattled off what she'd written on the notepad fast enough to make his head spin.

"You'll need to apply for permits."

"I'll head to city hall tomorrow. I want to start as soon as possible. Can you find a crew to do the work and purchase horses?"

"Yes." He felt pretty sure he could get her the horses from the Rocking W. That way, he'd know they were of good stock. "Do you want the attic done after the old barn?"

"Yes." She grinned. "This is exciting. The Willow Ridge Inn is going to be something spectacular. Grandma would be pleased."

"I agree." His phone dinged, signaling a text. He glanced at the screen to see a text from his friend. *Garrett Boyd is a real estate developer who is always looking for the next big thing. He's filed bankruptcy several times after work was done to avoid paying for the job. I'd advise against doing business with him.*

He read the text out loud. "Good thing you turned him down."

Bella frowned. "He sounds unscrupulous but not dangerous."

"Men hungry for money can be very dangerous."

Chapter Four

The next morning, Bella continued her read through the journal as she sipped her morning coffee. A deputy had brought it by the evening before, but he didn't let her know the sheriff's thoughts about what he'd read.

She set the mug down with a thunk, spilling some of the liquid inside when the words "decades-old-secret" involving the Davidson family jumped out at her.

This could be the clue behind what happened to her grandmother. Bella didn't know the Davidson family, but it wouldn't be hard to find out about them. Not in Misty Hollow where everyone seemed to know everyone's business.

Grandma went on to write about a cover-up from the 1970s. Scattered notes about strange occurrences and whispered conversations of guests over the years. Her grandmother's notes seemed cautious, as if she were afraid to write down too much, but she repeated *"incident"*; *"It was never supposed to get out"*; *"kept in the family"*; and other such disturbing comments.

Closing the journal, Bella straightened in her chair

and nibbled on a piece of buttered toast. The sheriff had to have the same suspicions she did, especially now. Should she trust him to follow through, or should she keep searching for answers herself?

Her gaze landed on her to-do list. She still had a lot to do before opening the inn to guests, something she hoped to do on Monday. That gave her less than a week to get things ready. She'd have to interview a gardener and a cook, plus she wanted to do some more cleaning out of the attic. Until she hired someone to clean the guest rooms, Bella could handle that job for now.

Excitement leaped in her heart. She was really doing this. Bella would make the inn everything her grandmother had dreamed of and more. No big resort would change that.

After she cleaned up from breakfast, Bella stashed the journal back into the roll-top desk, then climbed to the attic. She'd already started three piles—keep, throwaway, and donate. The largest pile was the keep one. She'd really need to be ready to let her grandmother's things go if she wanted to turn the attic into suites.

After an hour of digging through battered, dusty trunks, she found a small, locked wooden box. It wasn't hard to break into because the wood around the lock had splintered. Expecting to find old jewelry, Bella was surprised to see a collection of old, yellowed letters addressed to Mildred before she'd taken over the running of the inn.

The letters were from someone named Albert who had once worked at the inn during the 70s. At first, he filled her in on daily upkeep of the inn, but one of his letters almost made Bella's heart stop beating. Albert wrote about a tragic accident that had occurred one summer night in 1972. He described hearing screams, followed by the departure of a black car in the middle of the night. The next day there was no mention of the accident, and he was warned never to speak of it again.

"I don't know what happened to her that night," Albert wrote. *"But they buried the truth with her."*

Who was her? Bella dug deeper into the letters until she found a name. Emily Marks. Albert wrote in another letter that it had been rumored that she was involved with Henry Davidson, the mayor at that time, but no one could prove anything. When her body had been found near the Misty River, rumors were shut down.

"Bella?" Deacon's voice came up the attic stairs.

"Up here." She set the last letter on top of the ones she'd already read.

"What are you doing?"

"I found some letters to my grandmother from someone who used to work here before she took over. Have you ever heard of an Emily Marks?"

"No, but I didn't grow up here." He sat cross-legged beside her. "Why?"

"Seems she died under suspicious circumstances on this property." She motioned to the letters. "These letters will give us a clue as to why my grandmother was killed."

He arched a brow and reached for a letter. "Mind if I read them?"

"Go ahead. It's all very intriguing." She smiled and returned to the ones left in front of her. What if that long ago Davidson killed Emily and covered it up? If Grandma found out something to incriminate him, then his family might have come after her. The Davidson family was a prominent one. They wouldn't want their name sullied.

She mentioned it to Deacon.

"It's possible." He kept his gaze on the paper in his hand. "This Albert knew a lot about what went on around here. How many more letters are there?"

"Only a few, but there's a larger envelope at the bottom of this box." She pulled it out to discover it full of newspaper articles on the death of Emily Marks. She moved to Albert's last letter and read it aloud.

"I can't live with what I know. They'll come for me if I say more. Be careful, Miss Harper. It's not just about the past—it's about what's still happening."

~

"We need to find out more about this Albert and Emily Marks." Deacon reached for the news articles. "There's a Ms. June Mayfield that has been around for a long time. I bet she can tell us something. I could take you for supper to the diner, then stop by her place. She's always home and eager for visitors."

He returned his attention to the newspaper and quickly scanned the articles. Little was written other than the body of Emily Marks had been found in the river, and that Henry Davidson expressed a deep sadness for her family. Deacon slid the papers back in the envelope. "Let's go. The diner is a popular place, but it gets crowded."

Bella stood and dusted off her jeans. Without thinking, Deacon reached over and brushed a cobweb from her platinum hair. Her azure eyes widened in surprise.

"Sorry." He wasn't sorry in the least. Her hair had

felt like silk through his fingers. "Cobweb."

She nodded and rushed down the stairs. By the time he followed, she'd ducked into the bathroom. Ghost waited obediently outside the door, the dog's dark eyes fixed on Deacon.

"You want to go get a burger, boy?"

The dog let out a soft woof.

"Of course, he does." Bella, her hair now in a ponytail, stepped into the hall. "He lives for food."

In the truck, she asked, "Are you sure this Mayfield lady can help us?"

"If anyone knows anything, it's her." He nodded and drove to the diner where they once again sat at a table near the window so Bella could keep her eye on Ghost in the truck.

"The more I find in my grandmother's things, the more positive I am that someone murdered her," Bella said.

The waitress paused, eyes wide, then came to their table to take their orders. When she left, Deacon leaned forward. "Maybe we shouldn't talk about this here."

"Oh. Right." She gave a sheepish smile and glanced around the diner. "There are a few people who seem interested in our conversation."

They switched to discussing plans for the inn. When they'd finished, Bella carried a burger to her dog, then they drove to June's Victorian home.

The older woman sat rocking on the front porch, pushing to her feet as they parked in front. "Bring the dog with you. No sense for it to stay in the car. I've cookies and sweet tea. Come on in." She beckoned them with a smile and, leaning heavily on a purple, sparkly cane, went in her house.

"I like her already." Bella held the truck door open so Ghost could jump out.

"June's very well-liked by the folks in this town. She was born here and never left."

When they entered the house, June had already placed cookies and tea on the table. "I love visitors even if they only come to me for information. I'm a regular encyclopedia of Misty Hollow." She laughed and motioned them to sit at the table.

Bella offered her hand. "Isabella Harper. People call me Bella."

"I knew your grandmother. Horrible thing what happened to her."

Bella sat. You don't believe the heart attack story?"

"Heck no. Mildred was as strong as a horse." She took a sip of her tea, then added more sugar.

Deacon took a sip and almost gagged on the sweetness. "What can you tell us about the death of Emily Marks in the 70s?"

"Sweet girl, but a bit on the wild side. Folks around here thought she was messing around with the mayor. No one could prove anything, and the mayor's wife quashed any rumors she heard." June pursed her lips. "Why are you wanting to know about something that happened so long ago?"

He explained about the letters Bella had found. "They were written by someone named Albert."

She nodded. "He worked for the Harpers as groundskeeper and all-around handyman. Decent sort of fellow if I recollect correctly."

Deacon felt pretty sure she recollected everything just fine.

"There were conflicting witness accounts, police reports that seemed too neat, and talk about hush money to key folks in this town. Again, all speculation, but I'm on the side that Emily was killed to keep someone's dirty secret." June crossed her arms. "Same as Mildred."

Deacon shared a startled glance with Bella. "Anything to help us find out the truth?"

June leaned forward. "Let's just say that Tom Davidson, son of Henry, seems to have inherited his father's political ambitions. And his ruthlessness. He wants to run for mayor next election. I doubt he'd be happy having the past dug up whether he was running or not."

"Why be worried if there was never any proof?" Bella asked.

"Because even rumors are based on fact somewhere. It would raise questions in the minds of these folks and might influence their vote." She frowned. "Aren't you going to have a cookie? Oatmeal chocolate chip."

Despite being full from supper, he snatched one from the plate and bit it in half. "Still warm."

"Made them this evening. I never know who is going to pay me a visit, but someone does most nights. People think they need to check on me as if I can't take care of myself." She shook her head. "Makes me wonder how I've lived to be eighty-six."

Deacon laughed. "You'll reach a hundred."

"Wouldn't that be something?" She slapped her leg and cackled. "Only the good Lord knows the number of my days." She sobered and turned to Bella. "Mildred knew something. You find out what, and you'll find her killer."

Bella stood. "I intend to do just that. Thank you, Ms. Mayfield."

"Everyone calls me June, dear." She pushed to her feet. "Deacon, you watch over this girl. Trouble came to Mildred, so it's bound to come to her, too."

"I will, ma'am. Thank you for the tea and cookies."

"You're welcome." She patted Ghost on the head. "Y'all come back, you hear? I want to know all about what's going on at the inn."

Bella quickly filled her in as they moved to the porch. "Do you think Grandma would be happy with the changes?"

"Tickled pink." June cupped Bella's cheek. "Stay safe, girl. Find justice for my friend. I don't have many left."

"I will. I promise."

"Good. Now go find a killer."

Chapter Five

The next morning, Bella sat across the kitchen table from a man in worn, denim coveralls. He looked well past retirement age but insisted he wanted to work. That doing so would keep him on the living side of the earth. Despite his age, he looked capable of caring for the grounds. She stood and offered him her hand. "You're hired, Mr. Jones. When can you start?"

"You said I can fix me a place to live above the garage?"

"Yes, sir. There's electricity, water, a small kitchenette, and a bathroom." The small apartment had been a surprising and welcome find for Bella.

"Then as soon as I put my few belongings there." He gave her hand a vigorous shake.

"Great. You'll find your daily to-do list on a whiteboard in the barn." One down, one more to go. From the sound of gravel crunching out front, her next interview for a cook had arrived. So far, she'd struck out with the two she'd already interviewed.

Mr. Jones headed out the back door while Bella moved to greet the newest arrival on the porch. A middle-aged woman who barely hit five feet tall and almost as round bustled up the walk. "I'm Ida Coffman." Her smile lit up her round face.

"Nice to meet you. I'm Bella Harper. Please come in." Bella held the door open for her. "Can I get you some coffee? Tea?"

"Nothing for me, sweetie." The woman sat in one of the kitchen chairs and slid a fluorescent pink folder across the table. "Here's my resume. You said the job comes with room and board?"

"Yes, ma'am, and Sundays off." She opened the folder to see the woman had worked in a bed and breakfast for twenty years. "Why did you leave?"

"The owner died, and the son sold off the place to some real estate developer. It's a resort now."

Same thing Boyd wanted to do to the Willow Ridge. Bella pushed the thought away and continued with the interview. "Breakfast would be continental style, lunch a sandwich buffet, and supper an actual served meal. You okay with that?"

Ms. Coffman folded her arms across her ample bosom. "How many guests does the inn hold?"

"There are six rentals. I'm renovating the attic into two full-time suites. We have a gardener and a part-time handyman. I'll be hiring someone to care for the horses once I purchase them." *Please say you want the job.* Bella was more than ready to be done with the interviews.

"I can easily handle that."

"You're hired. Until guests start arriving, there will be only three or four of us. Let me show you to your room." Bella led her to a small room off the kitchen she'd turned into a bedroom. It wasn't much, but Ms. Coffman would have the run of the entire inn.

"This is perfect. I'll be back tomorrow with my things." She stopped at the front door and turned. "I'm excited to work in a place with such history."

"You know the history?"

"This inn used to be the envy of bed and breakfast owners throughout the state. The murder of that young girl in the 70s only increased the draw. You start letting folks know the place is open, and you'll be full in no time." Her eyes twinkled. "Some say the ghost of that girl haunts the place. You haven't seen her ghost, have you?"

"Of course not." Ghosts weren't real. "The only ghost around here is my dog."

Her new cook laughed and, for such a plump woman, moved quickly to her car. With a wave of her fingers, she climbed in and drove off leaving Bella free to do the next thing on her list. Visit the library and find out everything she could about the Donaldson family and the inn. She left a note for Deacon that she'd be back by dark, she hoped, and if he was hungry to help himself to anything in the fridge. She also told him about Rufus Jones and Ida, so he wouldn't be surprised.

Leaving Ghost to guard the place, she drove to the library. The Willow Ridge wasn't high on Misty Mountain, but it did have enough switchbacks that Bella definitely didn't want to drive the road in the dark. Gathering clouds overhead promised night would come early.

The librarian frowned when Bella told her what she was searching for. "I don't remember that murder. I didn't live here then, but we've had plenty of things make the news in the last few years." She typed on her keyboard. "We do have some floppy discs that haven't been uploaded on our new system. Let me show you where the ancient computer is."

The woman led her to a back room where a monstrosity from decades ago sat on a desk. "Those boxes over there are labeled by year. Just stick the disc there—" she pointed to a slot. "And read to your heart's content. If you want to print anything out, it's a dime a page. Let me know if I can be of further assistance."

"Thank you." Bella sat and started inserting disc after disc. She read about Donaldson becoming mayor, the inn winning an award for best in the state, and a small mention of Emily Marks' death. No word of who might have killed her. Her death became a cold case. She'd learned more in Albert's letters.

A glance at her watch sent her scurrying through the pouring rain to her car. It hadn't seemed like hours, but she'd spent far too much time in the archives.

As she turned onto the road leading up the mountain, headlights flashed behind her. Where had the truck come from? She hadn't spotted it earlier, then all of a sudden it rounded the corner and was following way too close.

The driver definitely seemed impatient and made as if to pass her, swerving dangerously close to her car. The roar of the engine rose above the clicking of Bella's windshield wipers.

She slowed down. The truck did the same. Her gaze shot to the upcoming curve. If a car came from the other direction, the truck would have no choice but to pull back or push her off the road.

Heart in her throat, Bella tightened her grip on the steering wheel. Another set of headlights came toward them.

The truck beside her slammed into her car. Bella screamed as her car went over the embankment and slammed into the trunk of a massive oak tree. Her airbags deployed. She fought herself free and stared in horror out the window. The tree had kept her from plummeting to the valley below. How was she going to climb to safety?

"Bella!"

Had someone called her name? She unhooked her seatbelt and turned in her seat, freezing when the car shuddered.

"Hold on. I'm coming to get you."

She released the breath she was holding. Deacon would save her. He must have been in the vehicle coming from the opposite direction.

~

When Deacon had seen Bella's car go off the road, his heart sped up. The black truck on big tires hadn't even stopped. What had the driver been thinking? Everyone knew not to pass on a sharp curve.

He uncoiled a length of rope from the bed of his truck and tied one end around his waist. He secured the other end to the bumper.

The rain made his descent down the embankment slippery and dangerous. One false move could send both him and Bella into the valley.

"Deacon!"

"I'm coming." He grabbed the trunk of a sapling with one hand and the car door handle with the other. "I'm going to pull you out. Whatever you do, don't let go of my hand. Okay?"

She nodded, eyes wide.

It took some yanking during which he felt sure the car would continue its descent before he got the door open. He reached in. "Take my hand."

She hung her purse around her neck, gripped his hand, and slid from the car.

"Don't look down." He kept a tight grip on the rope and on her.

"Too late." She pulled her hand free and gripped his belt. "It'll be easier for you to pull us up if you can use both your hands. Don't worry. I won't let go."

The use of both hands did make climbing up the slippery slope easier. By the time they reached his truck, they were both soaked and covered with mud. He helped Bella into the cab of his truck and handed her the blanket he kept behind the seat. "Are you hurt?"

"I'll be bruised from the seatbelt and airbags, but other than that...no. Did you see the truck?"

"Yes." He clenched his teeth. "Idiot driver."

"No, Deacon. He ran me off the road on purpose." She wrapped the blanket around her. "He followed me from the library."

He frowned. "Are you sure?"

"Positive."

"Then we're headed to town to speak to the sheriff." Rather than find a place to turn around and take her home, he drove to the sheriff's office where the receptionist took one look at them and told them to go on back.

Sheriff Westbrook listened, his face expressionless, as Bella recounted the accident.

"Can you describe the truck?"

"Black on big tires," Deacon said. "I didn't catch a glimpse of the license plate. I was more focused on getting to Bella."

The sheriff nodded. "I'll put out a BOLO for a vehicle matching that description and send someone in the morning to retrieve your car."

Bella's shoulders slumped. "It isn't worth retrieving. I'll need a new one."

"We'll get it anyway. The local mechanic, Roy, usually has one or two vehicles for sale. Go home and dry off, ma'am. I'll keep you updated on the truck."

He didn't sound like he thought they'd find the driver, Deacon thought. He'd keep a lookout himself. Heaven help the driver when he did.

Back at the inn, he sent Bella to take a hot shower while he made coffee. His hand shook as he measured the coffee into the filter. When he'd arrived at the inn to care for Blaze, he'd seen her note. He hadn't grown concerned until the rain, then the night both fell. Thinking she might've had car trouble, he'd gone looking for her. The last thing he'd expected to see was her plummeting off the mountain.

"Your turn." Bella, wearing a thick robe and a towel wrapped around her hair, joined him in the kitchen.

"I don't have any dry clothes here. I'll head back to the ranch if you're going to be all right." He didn't want to leave her so soon after her ordeal.

"I'll be fine. Rufus is over the garage, and Ghost won't leave my side." She smiled at the dog who stared up at her. "Unless the phantom ghost decides to pay a visit."

"What?" He frowned and poured her a cup of coffee.

"Ida said some folks think Emily's ghost haunts

the inn." After she accepted the cup, he turned to pour himself one.

He took a sip. "I haven't heard that one before."

"Good thing I don't believe in ghosts." She tilted her head and grinned. "My grandmother has a fuzzy yellow robe that might fit you."

"No, thanks." He laughed. "I'd rather stand here and shiver." He glanced at the back door. "If there is money in your budget, it might not be bad to install an alarm system."

"I thought of that, but then I'd have to give the guests the code and change it every time a new guest came. Ghost will have to be my warning system."

"Then at least install cameras."

"That I can do." She exhaled heavily. "I wish all I had to worry about was a phantom. Living people are far more dangerous, and tonight proved that someone will do anything to get me out of Misty Hollow. One way or another."

That thought scared Deacon to his core.

Chapter Six

Maybe it was the rumors of a ghost that had Bella on edge all night. She felt as if someone watched her sleep. A nightmare spun through her mind like a stuck record—one where she missed the huge oak tree and flew into the valley below the mountain. She jerked awake before hitting the ground.

Now, hands wrapped around a cooling cup of coffee, eyes gritty from lack of sleep, she tried to focus on the day's to-do list. Advertising that The Willow Ridge Inn was open again.

Ghost's deep barks drew her to the window. Two construction trucks filled with workers pulled up to where the barn would be made into an event venue. She smiled through her tiredness. With that crew, the place would be ready in no time. She'd add that to her marketing plan.

Rufus drove a riding lawnmower across the grounds. He'd already erected a new trellis for the morning glories and clematis climbing around the porch. Her new gardener had been busy at an early hour.

"Eat." Ida set a plate of scrambled eggs and bacon

on the table. "A strong wind could blow you away."

Bella had heard that her whole life. She'd been called Tinkerbell more times than she could count. "Thank you." A lot of those same people came to discover she was stronger than she looked.

She carried her breakfast to her office to eat while she set up the advertising. Several times while she worked, she glanced at the window, the hair on the back of her neck standing on edge. She shrugged off the feeling of being watched. The grounds around the inn bustled with activity. No doubt one of the workers had simply glanced through the window as he passed.

The scuff of a shoe sounded overhead. Bella frowned. She'd already made her bed. Had Ida gone to see what else needed doing?

A thump sent her running up the stairs. She almost collided with Ida who stepped from one of the guest rooms, her arms full of linens.

"Gracious, Bella."

"I'm sorry. Were you just in my room?"

"No, ma'am. You said you would take care of your own room." She tilted her head. "Why?"

"No reason." Bella passed her but stopped in her doorway. Nothing looked out of place other than the book she'd read before falling asleep. It now lay on the floor. Her glance went to the open bedroom window. It would've taken a very strong breeze to blow the book to the floor.

She replaced the book on her nightstand and stood at the window. She couldn't see anyone other than the workers, and they weren't close to the house. Nerves on edge, she checked the closet and the bathroom. Not finding anything else amiss, she returned to her office and tried to push away the feeling of being watched. Who wouldn't think that after almost being run off the mountain?

"Mail." Ida set a stack of envelopes on Bella's desk an hour later. "I'm making sandwiches for the workers. Chicken salad. Want one?"

"That sounds delicious." She appreciated the fact that she didn't have to micromanage either of her new staff members. They saw what needed doing and did it.

"After lunch, I'm headed to town for groceries. If there's something you want, let me know. We don't have enough right now for me to keep feeding the workers." Ida wiped her hands on her apron.

"No problem. Get what you need." *Thank you, Grandma, for leaving a healthy bank account.*

The mail consisted of a few bills, some junk mail, and a letter from Garrett Boyd. With a grimace, she opened the envelope and pulled out the thick sheet of stationery.

My Dear Miss Harper:

I have the opportunity to make a bid on another piece of property and wanted to give you one more chance at selling. Why not keep the money in your account rather than someone else's? Please reconsider and let me know. I'll be signing papers on the other land in three days.

Sincerely,
Garrett Boyd.

"Go ahead and sign. I'm not changing my mind,"

she wrote back. Instead, she'd give his fancy resort a run for its money. She offered something he wouldn't. Clean, honest fun and an at-home atmosphere at more reasonable prices than Boyd could offer at an expensive resort.

Satisfied with the work she'd done on marketing, Bella made one more sweep through the house to make sure she didn't need to order anything else in order to be ready for guests, then stepped outside.

The rat-a-tat of hammers and nail guns filled the air, drawing her eyes to the bustle of activity. An awning had been erected over the barn door. Men worked like an army of ants replacing shingles on the roof.

As she walked the perimeter of the building, her mind whirled with possibilities. A bench there, a fountain there, flowers and blooming shrubs over there. Behind the barn, a pond shimmered in the early afternoon sun. There were plenty of beautiful spots for a wedding or photo shoots.

She pulled her cell phone from her pocket and snapped a few pictures to use in her advertising. Convinced she'd soon be hosting events, she turned back to the house...and froze. A face appeared in the attic window, then withdrew.

"Ghost, come." She sprinted for the house and thundered up the stairs, bursting into the attic. An empty expanse greeted her, other than a few boxes she still needed to go through.

She'd seen someone. Her mind wasn't playing tricks. She'd heard footsteps in her bedroom and now this. Maybe the ghost of Emily Marks was real. No, the face she'd seen in the window had been a man's. A human was playing games with her.

~

"Anyone home?" Deacon called out.

"Be right there." Bella joined him in the foyer a few minutes later. Worry creased her brow.

"What's wrong?"

"Nothing." She took a deep breath. "What's up?"

"I found out some more information on Boyd. Do you have time?"

"Yes. I also received a letter from him today. I'll meet you in the kitchen. Ida is making lunch." She headed down the stairs, then stopped, one hand on the banister, and faced him. "You're early today."

He grinned. "Just making a pit stop while out running errands."

She nodded and continued down the stairs then turned toward her office, while he headed for the kitchen. "Howdy, ma'am."

The cook turned. "You aren't one of the workers."

"No, ma'am. I'm the part-time handyman, Deacon Simpson."

"Have a seat, Deacon Simpson, and I'll make you a sandwich. I'm Ida." She turned back to the counter where pieces of bread were lined up like an assembly line. Her efficiency reminded him of Mrs. White, the cook at the ranch.

"Can I ask you something?" He perched on a bar stool.

"Sure." She continued making sandwiches.

"Does Bella seem spooked to you?"

"She has been a bit preoccupied. I assumed it was because of all the commotion around here. Why?" She glanced over her shoulder.

He told her about the truck trying to run her off the mountain the night before. "Did she mention that to you?"

"Not a word." Her forehead creased. "She doesn't know me well enough to confide in me."

"Hmm." He turned as Bella entered the kitchen. "Is it okay to talk in here?" He gave a subtle nod of his head toward Ida.

Bella nodded and handed him a letter. "Have you heard of a large plot of land up for sale?"

"No."

"Neither have I," Ida said. "And I know just about everything there is to know around here. The man is trying to get you to cave." She returned to putting cheese on top of the bread.

"What did you find out?" Bella glanced at the ceiling and bit her bottom lip.

"The Boyd family is known for bullying landowners into selling, often using unscrupulous means to coerce them to sell. He's close friends with Mayor Raney and the Davidson family. Those three are the trifecta of trouble around here wanting to turn Misty Hollow into a resort town."

"That's why he wants your land, Bella." Ida started packing the sandwiches into a basket. "You've got prime real estate, and he thinks you're an easy target. Might also have something to do with the secret from a long time ago."

"Emily Marks?" Deacon widened his eyes.

"No. Prohibition money. This is an old house. Some say there's money hidden in the walls." She wiggled her eyebrows, the gesture making her cheeks bounce.

Deacon shook his head. "I've ripped down walls in this house. Other than a few hidden passages between rooms—"

"Hidden passages?" Bella paled.

"Didn't your grandmother told you about them? I figured you'd have played in these walls as a child."

"No, she didn't." She glanced upward again. "Deacon, I've been hearing footsteps on the second floor today and saw a man in the attic window." Her worried gaze returned to him. "I thought it was nerves because of yesterday. Now, I'm positive someone is using those passages to move around in."

Ida handed Deacon a sandwich.

"I'll eat this on the run, ma'am. Bella, I'll be back later to install those cameras. We'll need some in the hallways in addition to outside." He slid from the stool. "Keep Ghost close." He put a hand on her shoulder. "Don't worry. I won't let anything happen to you. We'll find out who is behind these games and stop them."

Worry clouded her eyes. She shoved her hair out of her face. "Thank you."

Deacon rushed back to the ranch to finish his work for the day, eager to get back to the inn to install the cameras. He'd have to stop at the mercantile for a few more, which would put him back at the inn after supper. He'd be pushing it to install the cameras before dark.

"You've sure been driving a path in the mountain." His boss, Dylan, met him in the garage. "I know you've been helping at the inn. Is there trouble?"

"Yep." Deacon sighed and filled his boss in on what was happening.

"Why not take a week off and try to put an end to

the trouble?" Dylan cocked his head. "We've enough hands for a bit. Two new hires are starting tomorrow."

"You sure?"

"Absolutely." His boss grinned. "New women always bring trouble to Misty Hollow. It's a curse. Watch your heart. The men who help these women always end up falling for them."

"Not me." Deacon had goals to own land of his own. He couldn't let a woman derail what he'd worked so hard for.

"Sure." Laughing, Dylan headed for the main house, then stopped. "Oh, forgot to tell you the horses you bought will arrive in the morning. If you need help transporting them, grab one of the other hands."

"Thanks." Bella would be pleased. Each day ticked another item off her list for the inn. Too bad Mildred couldn't see the transformation for herself.

Once he'd finished his work, Deacon made a quick run to the mercantile for more cameras. On his return trip to the inn, he kept an eye on his rearview mirror expecting to see the big black truck. He scanned parking lots and driveways on his way out of town. He'd find the truck—of that he had no doubt, and the driver would pay for almost killing Bella.

When he returned to the inn, construction had stopped for the day and the workers were gone. Good. He didn't want a lot of folks knowing there were now security cameras. If someone was moving through the secret passages, he'd be easier to catch if he didn't know about the cameras.

Chapter Seven

Days later while cleaning out the attic, Bella discovered more letters from Albert to her grandmother. Brimming with a sense of accomplishment at ticking off a huge task from her to-do list, she carried the last box from the attic to her office. She had a few hours before she needed to go to city hall to fill out the form that had slipped her mind for the current renovations.

She sat cross-legged on the floor of her office and started reading. These letters focused more on the death of Emily Marks. Not only did Davidson's name come up several times, but also the name of the current mayor, Robert Raney. Best buddies during the day, according to Albert.

Bella had only met the man once. He'd seemed like another Garrett Boyd—smile too big, hair too perfect—Her hand shook with the next letter.

Albert mentioned a "reckless night" of drinking and partying which involved Robert and Davidson's fathers. Bella's grandmother had made some notations on the letter about looking into a more solid connection between the two families. If she'd succeeded, then Bella had stumbled onto the motive for her grandmother's death.

These letters needed to be hidden. She scrambled to her feet and retrieved the others from her desk. Where could she put them where no one would think to look?

At first, she thought of putting them into a plastic bag and slipping it into the toilet tank, but she quickly discarded that idea. A cliché hiding place from too many books. Same as a false drawer in a desk. The secret passages were also a no since someone was getting into her house that way.

"Where, Ghost?"

Her dog woofed.

"Good idea. The barn should have plenty of hiding places. No one could go in or out of there without you seeing them." She shoved all the letters into one box and carried them to the barn which now housed five other horses in addition to Blaze.

Before entering, she glanced around for the young man, JD something, that Deacon had hired for her. Not seeing him, she ducked into the barn. Soft nickers and the scent of hay greeted her. She stood right inside the doorway and scanned the area for a place to hide the box.

A set of wooden stairs led to the second floor which was now used as storage since the former house was no longer a place of residence except for the horses. That would be too obvious.

It could be that no one would ever come looking for the letters. Quite possible no one knew about them now that Albert and her grandmother were gone. At least, she suspected Albert had to have passed by now. Still, she wasn't taking any chances.

Her gaze fell on a shovel. She'd dig a hole under the outside water spigot. No one would think of looking under something used on a regular basis.

Once she had the box wrapped in a waterproof tarp and buried, she hurried to the house to clean up, then drove her new car to town. She parked behind the courthouse and headed inside and up the stairs. Filling out forms was such a waste of time. She turned the corner and collided with a man in a suit. Robert Raney.

"Whoa, little lady. What's your hurry?" He narrowed his eyes and smoothed his suit jacket.

"I need to fill out some forms before the office closes. Excuse me." She took a step to the side to brush past him.

"You're Mildred Harper's granddaughter, aren't you?" He gave a big grin. "Heard there are all kind of changes going on at the inn."

"Yes, sir." She pasted on a smile and took another step toward the office.

"I'll have to come out and see someday."

"You do that. Excuse me."

"See you around, Miss Harper." The mayor's tone grew cool.

Bella stiffened, but tried not to react. Instead, she shoved open the door to the office and requested the proper forms. Had he just made a threat? She didn't know the mayor well enough, but his words hung in the air.

Bella needed to talk to someone who might know more about Emily Marks. She and Deacon had already talked to June Mayfield. Who else might know something?

She handed the completed forms to the clerk and

paid the fee. "Who in Misty Hollow was here in the 70s?"

The girl looked at her with surprise. "June Mayfield."

"Other than her."

The clerk scrunched up her mouth. "Um…Fred Murphy, I think. He owns the mercantile. Then, there are a couple of old guys who hang around the diner a lot, but I don't recall their names."

"Thank you." Bella hurried back to her car. As she backed from her spot, she spotted Raney watching her from a second-story window. She returned his stare for a couple of seconds, then drove to the mercantile.

Inside, she pretended to browse while Fred helped a customer. When the man left with a box of nails, Bella approached the counter. "Mr. Murphy?"

"Miss Harper."

She frowned. "How did you know my name?"

"Everyone knows about Mildred's granddaughter. She spoke about you a lot. Besides, the work you're doing on the inn is the talk of the town." He crossed his arms. "What do you need?"

"Some answers, I hope." She smiled. "Do you remember an Albert that used to work at the inn in the 70s?"

His eyes narrowed. "Everyone knew Albert. Why?"

"He mentioned to my grandmother about something that happened back then. Something about a girl named Emily Marks. Do you know anything about her?"

His eyes flitted to hers then away. "A wild girl. Switched from one boy to the next like a moth." He turned and started straightening items on a shelf behind him. "I'm busy."

Bella would not be deterred. "I read in an old newspaper article that her body was found in the river. I also read there was some speculating about the fathers of Raney and Davidson."

He whipped around. "You read no such thing."

Her smile widened. "Why would that be, Mr. Murphy? Because something happened that the town has hushed up? Or because people are afraid of the Raneys and Davidsons? What did those young men do to Emily?"

His eyes narrowed. "Leave things be, Miss Harper. Please. You don't know what you're sticking your nose into."

"I think I do. My grandmother had discovered something, and that something got her killed." She slapped the counter. "It was no heart attack that killed her, and I aim to prove it." She took a deep breath to regain her self-control. "If you know something that let a guilty person walk free, then you might as well have killed Emily and my grandmother yourself!" She stormed from the store to see Deacon climbing out of his truck.

A wide grin spread across his face, then faded. "What's wrong?"

~

"That man knows something."

"Fred?"

"Yes. I asked him about Albert, Emily, Raney and Davidson." She crossed her arms. "He told me to stay out of things."

Deacon took her by the elbow and led her away

from the store. "What did you find out?"

"From him?" She jerked her head. "That he knows something and won't talk. I found out more than that from some other letters I found in the attic."

He glanced at the mercantile where Fred watched from the door. "Let's grab a bite to eat at Lucy's. Call Ida and tell her we won't be there for supper because we're having a late lunch."

"I'm not hungry." She glared over her shoulder at Fred.

"I am, and it will give us a chance to talk." He led her to her car. "Meet me there?"

"Fine." She climbed into the driver's seat, eyes flashing as she shot another glare toward the mercantile.

Man, she was cute when riled. Chuckling, Deacon stepped out of the way as she squealed tires leaving the parking lot.

"Stop her from nosing around, Deacon," Fred warned. "She's going to get herself in trouble."

Deacon waved a hand, then climbed back into his truck. Yes, Bella might be putting herself in trouble, but he also knew he couldn't stop her. All he could do was his best to keep her safe.

Bella waited for him outside the diner. "I'm so mad I could spit nails."

"I can see that." He put a hand on the small of her back and guided her inside. "Don't say anything until we're seated." He smiled at the hostess. "A back booth, please." It would provide a little more privacy than a table by the window.

After the server took their orders, a salad for Bella and a chicken fried chicken for him, he leaned against the back of the booth. "Now tell me what has you worked up."

She told about the letters she'd found, her run-in with Mayor Raney, and her time in the mercantile. "It definitely seems as if someone is covering up something, although the mayor didn't say anything threatening. He is involved. I know it. Not directly, of course, but his father was either involved in Emily's death or helped cover up what happened to her. Same with my grandmother." She slowly turned her glass of iced tea in the puddle of condensation on the table. "Nothing is going to stop me from proving my grandmother was murdered." She raised her gaze. "What do you know about Raney and Davidson?"

"Not much. I didn't grow up here." He glanced at the lunch counter where Wilbur Stillwell sat. "Wilbur might." He slid from the counter, then perched on a stool next to Wilbur. "I'm Deacon Simpson, and I'll buy your lunch if you'll join me and my friend and answer some questions."

The old man's brow lowered. "I know who you are. You work at the Rocking W. I also know that's Mildred's granddaughter, and she's nosing around. Since Mildred was my friend, I'll join you and let you buy my food." He slid from the stool and slid into the booth next to Bella.

"I don't know who killed Mildred."

Bella gasped. "You believe she was murdered?"

"Of course, she was. Sheriff Westbrook thinks so, too. He's looking into it and coming up empty."

Deacon shared a startled glance with her. "He didn't say anything."

"He wouldn't talk about an active investigation,

now would he?" Wilbur waved to let the counter girl know he's moved to the booth. "That would tip off the killer."

"Do you know who killed Emily Marks?" Bella asked.

"What makes you think she was killed?" Wilbur tilted his head.

"Letters I've read from an Albert to my grandmother."

Wilbur smiled. "That old coot managed to tell what he knew before dementia set in. Poor guy. He's gone now, of course."

"We figured." Deacon motioned for them not to say anything as their food was delivered. When the server left, he said, "What do you know about the night Emily died?"

"Why don't you think she was murdered?" Bella added.

He bit into his plain cheeseburger. "Emily, bless her soul, wasn't what one would call a good girl. On the night in question, there'd been a party at the lake behind the inn. Most of the young folks of this town had gone, me included." He dipped a fry in ketchup. "Lots of drinking going on. Someone brought a guitar. Reminded me of photos of parties I'd seen from the sixties." He sighed. "Emily started dancing. Kind of provocatively, if you ask me. Focused on the two rich boys in town. Robert Raney, father of the current mayor, and Henry Davidson, father of the current Hank Davidson. Those two boys were considered a catch, especially to a pretty gal from the wrong side of the tracks, so to speak." He met Deacon's gaze. "She'd do almost anything to get one of them to marry her, and I do mean anything."

"Can you be specific?" Bella asked.

"Well, rumor has it that she might've been pregnant by one of those two boys."

"Would one of them have killed her because she was pregnant?"

Wilbur shrugged. "They would've wanted to keep that quiet as much as she would've wanted it made public."

Deacon and Bella needed to dig deeper into the lives of the former Raney and Davidson. "Either of them still alive?"

"David is. Lives in the nursing home in Langley."

Chapter Eight

Ghost growled deep in his throat. Bella's eyes popped open when footsteps sounded overhead. Someone was in the attic.

Bella slipped out of bed and puther feet into soft-soled slippers. If someone was up there, the cameras would catch them. The authorities would finally know who crept inside her walls. "Come, Ghost," she whispered. No way was she going to the attic alone.

After a week of doors left ajar, scurry sounds in the walls, and footsteps at odd hours, she would put a stop to it right now. A bang of thunder, then the flash of lightning sent her heart into her throat. What a fitting night for a "phantom" intruder.

Another roll of thunder. Ghost cowered and leaned against her leg.

"It's okay, boy. Stay close." She grabbed an iron poker from the basket near the bedroom fireplace. "Let's catch a crook."

Heart racing, she stopped at the foot of the attic stairs and listened. Ghost's ears perked, and he looked toward one of the guest rooms. Was there a passage from the attic to the other rooms? She'd assumed the secret ways through the house were confined to the main part. Her heart skipped a beat. What if there were more than one person in her house?

Her hand sweated around the fireplace poker. She would be no match for two men, barely a match for one, even with Ghost at her side.

She backed away from the attic and moved downstairs, putting one foot in front of the other in order not to make any noise. When she reached the bottom, she locked herself and Ghost in her office. "Let's see who is in our house."

The screen of her laptop remained blank. She glanced at the modem sitting nearby. No lights blinked. Had the storm taken out the Wi-F? She punched a few buttons on her laptop. Nothing that needed the internet worked.

She wanted, no *needed*, to call Deacon, but her cell phone was on her nightstand. She glanced out the window toward the garage. No lights shone from Rufus's window. No lights on her end either, come to think of it. The only light illuminating her way was the moon outside.

"We're going out, boy." No way did she want to stay alone in a dark house. With Ida gone for the night, Bella would rather brave the storm then stay inside with someone creeping above in the passage.

Bella grabbed an umbrella from a painted metal milk barrel by the front door before stepping onto the front porch, leaving the door slightly ajar in case she needed to get in fast. She'd no sooner opened the umbrella than the wind whipped it from her hands. Rain pelted her face.

Maybe she overreacted by leaving the comfort of

her home to brave the storm, but she wasn't staying there with an unseen prowler within. Head down, she gripped Ghost's collar, more for comfort than anything else, and trudged through an already muddy lawn toward the garage.

She glanced upward as she rounded the corner of the inn. A light flickered in the attic. A flashlight? She increased her pace before whoever was up there saw her leaving.

Just because she was terrified didn't mean she'd give whoever plagued her the satisfaction of knowing they'd caused her to flee her home. She raced up the steps to the apartment over the garage and banged on the door. "Rufus!"

It took several bangs before the door opened. "Miss Harper?"

"Let us in, please." She pushed past him. "Someone is in the inn. Someone I don't know is sneaking around through the walls and in the attic."

"Want me to go take a look?" He grabbed a rifle from the wall over his television set.

"Would you? I can't call for help. I left my cell phone in my room." She sat on the sofa, keeping Ghost close.

"I got this, Miss Harper. Lock the door behind me." He slipped into the night.

Please, God, keep Rufus safe. Bella locked the door, then resumed her seat on the sofa, her gaze glued to the front door.

After what seemed like an eternity, Rufus returned carrying her cell phone. "I didn't see anyone, but I definitely heard noises. You're headed to Langley later, right?"

"Yes." She glanced at the time. One a.m. Deacon would pick her up in seven hours to pay the elder Davidson a visit at the nursing home. Plenty of time to catch some sleep.

"I'm going to head to the courthouse tomorrow, with your permission, and see if I can't get a hold of the blueprints to the inn. I hope to find the entrance to the secret passage by the time you return home."

"Thank you. Do you mind if I crash here?" The thought of returning home, knowing someone still moved between the walls, sent ice through her veins.

"Of course." He smiled and fetched her a blanket and pillow. "Sleep well, ma'am."

She did, waking up at six-thirty, and rushed back to the inn to get ready for the day. Ghost's barking as she showered told her Deacon had arrived.

"Bella?"

"Be down in a few." Towel wrapped around her, she raced for her bedroom. By the time she'd dressed and joined him downstairs, Rufus had filled him in on the night's events.

"Those cameras have battery backup," Deacon said. "Whatever they recorded should still be there after the Wi-Fi came back on. Let's take a look before we head out."

Bella and Rufus followed him to her office. A few minutes later, the three of them stared at a hooded, masked man in the attic. Another one popped into view, then moved out of the camera's range.

The intruders were searching for something. The letters to her grandmother? It seemed clear they weren't at the inn only to frighten Bella into leaving.

"They look too young to be Raney or Boyd." Bella

frowned. "Hired?"

"Most likely." Deacon copied the recording and sent it as an attachment in an email to the sheriff. "Let's see what Davidson can tell us. I also have a few weeks to help you through this. I'll be by in the morning to rent a room."

~

Blissful Acres, the Langley nursing home, was a squat, concrete block building nestled in between oak trees, rose bushes, and seasonal flowers. Deacon pressed a button by the entrance. The door swung open.

"Not a very secure place, is it?" Bella shook her head.

"Doesn't seem that way. Anyone could walk up and press that button."

Two women sat behind an oval counter. "May I help you?" One of them asked.

"We'd like to see Henry Davidson, please."

She slid a clipboard toward him. "Sign in here. He should be in the cafeteria having breakfast. For three dollars each, you can eat with him. Head down that hall and follow the signs. Don't expect too much. He slips in and out of lucidness."

No request to see identification or questions about why they wanted to visit one of the residents. Very lax security in his opinion. Deacon signed their names, then headed down the hall, matching his steps to Bella's.

They fell into line at the buffet after paying for the meal and asked which person was Davidson. The young man behind the buffet making to-order omelets, pointed out a wheelchair-bound man with hunched shoulders and gray hair sitting alone.

He lifted dark eyes as they sat at his table. "Do I

know you?"

"No, sir." Deacon smiled. "I'm Deacon Simpson and this is Isabella Harper. You may have known her grandmother, Mildred, owner of the Willow Ridge Inn. Isabella owns it now."

The man mumbled something about unfinished business and someone who was wronged. His hand shook as he reached for his glass of milk. "Yes, I knew Mildred."

"Did you know Emily Marks?" Bella tilted her head.

Milk sloshed over the rim of the glass as he set it down, hard, on the table. He dabbed at the spill with a napkin. "A long time ago."

"What happened the night she died, Mr. Davidson?" Bella reached over and finished wiping up the spilled milk. "Someone told us you were there."

He ducked his head, pushing his scrambled eggs around his plate. "I don't know. Like I said, it was a long time ago."

"It's hard to forget a tragedy, sir." Deacon took a bite out of a slice of bacon. Cold. He frowned and set it back on his plate.

"I don't remember a tragedy." He mumbled something Deacon couldn't decipher.

Deacon folded his hands on the table. "There was a party at the lake behind the inn. You, Robert Raney, Emily Marks, and others were there. Drinking was involved. Rumor has it that Emily had her eye on you and Raney. That she may have gotten pregnant in order to trap one of you into marriage. Know anything about that?"

"A loose girl. A liar," he muttered . "Secrets.

Vows." He shook his head.

They were losing him. "Was Emily pregnant? Were you or Raney the father?"

His head wagged from side to side, and he was starting to grow agitated. "Promises. She lied. She needed to be silenced."

"Who silenced her, Mr. Davidson?" Deacon leaned closer.

"Not a good girl. Not a good girl." He started to rock.

An aide rushed over. "Visit is over. Let me take you to your room, Mr. Davidson."

Deacon sighed and pushed to his feet. "Let me treat you to a real breakfast. I'm starved."

"It's obvious he knows exactly what happened to Emily." Back in his truck, Bella clicked her seatbelt into place. "I wonder whether he's had other visitors beside us."

Why hadn't he thought of that? "Wait here." He hurried back to the main doors and pressed the button. As the doors slid open, he slipped in sideways and made a beeline for the front desk. "Has Mr. Davidson had any other recent visitors?"

"The mayor of Misty Hollow comes once a month. He was here…" she flipped through the visitor registry. "Two days ago."

"Thank you." Deacon smiled and returned to his truck. "Raney was here two days ago. Wanna bet he warned Davidson not to say anything? Scared him into being silent?"

"That's a bet you'd win." She pursed her lips, the gesture doing funny things to his insides. "Now what? We can't exactly go up to the mayor and ask about him threatening the long-time friend of his father."

"No, we can't." He backed from the parking spot. "We do know that something happened with Emily that Davidson knows about. If he knows, then others do too. I'd guess someone other than Davidson or Raney. We need to find out who else would've gone to that party. Who Emily's friends were."

"Anyone living in Misty Hollow who are in their mid-sixties should know. Should we pay another visit to June?"

Deacon nodded. "We can ask her about anyone else still around from that time. June would've been too old to attend the party." He reached over and grasped her hand. "We're getting somewhere, Bella."

She smiled. "Hopefully, Rufus has news for us at the inn."

When they arrived, Rufus met them on the front porch, a grin across his face. "I have a few things to show you. The blueprints of the inn held a few surprises. Follow me."

He first led them to the old well house that sat not too far from the main house. Inside, he lifted a dirt-covered trapdoor. "This is one entrance. It leads to the closet under the stairs."

Bella's eyes widened. "I didn't know there was a door in that closet."

"Everything is very well hidden. I'll put a lock on the house. The other entrance is behind the barn in the old storm shelter."

He led them there and down the concrete steps into the storm shelter once used to hold canned goods. He pulled aside one of the shelving units. "There's a tunnel here that goes to the living room. A lever there pushes aside one of the bookcases."

He led them into a dark tunnel and pulled a flashlight from his pocket. Dirt walls held up by wood planks stretched in front of them. At the end, they stepped into the light of the living room.

"This is how your ghosts are getting in."

Chapter Nine

Bella slept better than she had in a long time. With locks on the passage entrances, no one could get in. If they tried to cut the lock, an alarm would sound, signaling law enforcement. She smiled and stretched, ready to face a day that would see the completion of the event venue. All she'd need to do was decorate, take photos, and increase her marketing.

She showered, dressed, then carried her laptop to the back deck with a cup of coffee made by Ida who had returned before the sun rose. With a satisfied grin, Bella gazed at the recently manicured flower garden her grandmother had once taken pride in, then she opened her laptop. Her email showed two reservations, a family wanting two rooms for the next week and one single.

Flesh and blood phantoms deterred, event venue nearing completion, now she could concentrate on her first guests. Nothing could mar the beauty of the morning.

Tires crunched out front. Except Garrett Boyd. He could mar the beauty of the morning.

With a sigh, Bella set her laptop and coffee down, then lumbered through the house to the front porch.

He strode toward her, his pace deliberate, his gaze locked on her. She shuddered at the coldness in his eyes. There was no sign of the businesslike charm he wore during his first visit. Today, his jaw was set with determination.

She crossed her arms and glared. "How can I help you, Mr. Boyd?" She braced herself to hear the reason for his visit.

"My dear Miss Harper." His voice carried an unsettled charm. While he kept his smile light, it felt more like a condescending threat than a greeting. "We need to talk."

She dug her nails into her arms. "There is nothing more to say, Mr. Boyd. The inn is not for sale."

His smile faded. "You're making a mistake. Your grandmother should have sold when she had the chance." He glanced around. "I see you've made some marvelous improvements. Unfortunately, I doubt someone with your lack of experience can carry this off. If you don't take this last offer, you'll be stuck with the inn. It's a burden I doubt you can afford to carry."

The words were a slap to the face. Not because she believed them, but because he had the audacity to tell her she couldn't manage the inn. "I. Am. Not. Selling. This inn has been in my family for generations, as has the land. I'm not going to let someone like you take it away."

"Someone like me?" His expression turned sinister, and he took a step forward. She instinctively stepped back. "You simply do not understand. This inn is not some family relic. It's a prime piece of real estate. You're standing in the way of some powerful men, Miss Harper. Same as your grandmother did. I promise you that you won't like what happens if you don't change your mind."

"Are you threatening me?" Her pulse quickened.

His lip curled. "I'm giving you a chance to walk away before things become...difficult. I've offered you more than this house is worth. Everyone has a breaking point, Miss Harper. I'm willing to bet you're no different."

Her breath came faster. Before she could respond, Deacon came around the corner of the house, a battered leather duffel bag in his hand.

"It's time for you to leave, Boyd." His eyes flashed. "Miss Harper has told you multiple times that she is not selling."

Bella had never been happier to see someone in her life. She grinned in Boyd's direction.

"You're going to regret this." The man sneered, then marched back to his car. As he put his hand on the door handle, he said, "I won't be back with another offer. Not the kind you want anyway."

"We will take that as a direct threat." Deacon made a move toward him. "Anything happens to us or this inn, and you will be held responsible."

"Are you threatening me?" Boyd arched a brow.

"No, sir. That is a promise."

By then, Rufus, armed with a rifle and Ida with an iron skillet joined her on the porch. Keith, the young man who took care of the horses, came around the corner and stood next to Deacon, a pistol in his hand.

"See, Mr. Boyd?" Bella grinned. "I am not alone here."

The man's face darkened and yanked his car door open. With a scowl, he climbed inside and spun gravel away from the inn.

Tears welled in Bella's eyes. "Thank you. All of you."

"We won't let that man get his hands on one rock of this land." Ida gave a definitive nod. "Not one single pebble."

The others expressed similar statements before drifting back to their jobs. Bella took a deep breath through her nose, then released it slowly out of her mouth. "Their support means everything to me."

Deacon dropped his bag and rushed up the steps, taking her in his arms and cradling her head against his chest. "They're good people. Boyd will get the hint and leave you alone."

"You don't think he's behind the break-ins?"

"No, I don't. He's nothing more than a blowhard. I think Raney and Davidson are behind everything else. They don't want to buy this place. They want their dirty deeds about what happened to Emily Marks kept secret."

~

The next morning, Deacon went looking for Bella to take her to town for some supplies she'd mentioned needing. He found her staring at what at once been her grandmother's garden.

"It's all gone." Tears poured down her face. "All Rufus's hard work."

Rose bushes crushed. Flowers trampled. Herbs and spices smashed under muddy footprints.

He frowned. "Did you hear anything last night?"

"A little, but Ghost didn't bark, so I thought maybe Rufus was doing patrol."

His chest tightened. This wasn't an act of

vandalism; it was a message. "Time to visit Sheriff Westbrook again."

"Yes." Her shoulders slumped. "This had to be Boyd. Let's take a look at the camera footage."

The footage showed a young man or a woman in a black hoodie. The culprit wisely kept their face averted which meant they knew the cameras had been installed. Deacon groaned inwardly. Without proof Boyd was behind the destruction, the sheriff didn't have anything to go on. And why hadn't Ghost barked?

He stood and moved through the kitchen to the doggy door. "Do you let Ghost roam the house at night?"

"Yes. He's a guard dog, sort of." She shrugged. "He's also a friendly one. We're training him to be more aggressive."

Deacon ran his fingers over a spot on the floor. "It's greasy. Would he eat something offered to him by a stranger?"

"I don't know. It's never happened before."

"It appears as if someone shoved a piece of meat through the doggy door to occupy Ghost. Just an assumption, but it makes sense. Let's close this off at night from now on." Placing his hands on his knees, he straightened. "Let's talk to the sheriff."

The sheriff's office was bustling when they arrived. A group of young teen boys had been caught drinking on a party boat in the middle of the lake.

The receptionist waved Deacon and Bella on back, stating the sheriff would be relieved to get a break from the gang of hooligans.

"Thank God." The sheriff exited an interrogation room and ushered them into his office where he slammed the door behind them. "Why weren't these kids in school?" He held up a hand. "I don't expect an answer. Sure will be glad when the new sheriff starts. She can deal with the crazies while I go fishing and enjoy my wife and children. Sit." He fell back into his chair.

Bella started right in about the destruction to her grandmother's garden and what they saw on the cameras. Deacon mentioned his suspicion that the dog had been otherwise engaged with a greasy piece of food.

When they finished, the sheriff reached for his phone. "Hudson, I'd like you to head over to the Willow Ridge Inn and take a look around. Too much is happening over there for us not to put it as a top priority." He hung up. "Deputy Hudson will meet you there. Once things settle down here, I'll send someone to talk to Boyd."

Deacon thanked him, then he and Bella= returned to his truck. Before Deacon had a chance to open the door for Bella, she rushed toward Boyd who was ambling up the sidewalk.

Deacon hurried to her side in time to hear Boyd say, "Nice garden."

"How would you know someone messed with her garden?" He narrowed his eyes.

"Word gets around. Probably spread by one of your employees." His voice dripped with mock sympathy. "It's a shame, really, but accidents like that can make someone reconsider their priorities, don't you think?"

"It wasn't an accident," Bella hissed. "I know you had something to do with the vandalism."

"That would be hard to prove, Miss Harper." His gaze hardened. "You shouldn't make accusations you can't back up."

Bella crossed her arms. "I'll find a way to prove it. Believe me, I'm not afraid of you."

His smirk faded. "You should be. You have no idea what you're up against, Miss Harper. I always get what I want, and I want that inn. You can either sell it willingly or...well, things will get worse before they get better."

Deacon's blood boiled. "Making a threat like that can get you arrested."

"Not at all." Boyd turned his smile on Deacon. "Merely stating a fact. Not even a cowboy like you will keep me from getting that inn."

"We'll see." Deacon took Bella by the arm and ushered her back to the truck. "Don't provoke him. We have bigger things to deal with."

"Like what?" She yanked free.

"Digging into what happened to Emily Marks."

"Oh, right." She climbed into the truck. Once he joined her, she faced him. "How do we question Davidson and Richards?"

"That's what we need to figure out." He backed away from the sheriff's office as a deputy's car pulled out. "We need to meet the deputy at the inn. Then we'll come up with a plan after he leaves. Plus, we need to get a hold of Emily's yearbook. See who else might've been at that party."

"The school library might have a copy. I'll call and see if someone can bring one by." She looked up the number on her phone, then made the call. A couple of minutes later, she grinned. "A high school student will bring a copy by this afternoon."

"Good work." He reached over and patted her shoulder. "That ought to get us somewhere."

Deputy Hudson was leaning against his vehicle when they arrived. As they pulled alongside him, he pushed away from the car with a smile. "I took the liberty of going around back," he said once they exited the truck. "Whoever tore up the garden did a good job. I took some photos and told your man, Rufus, that he couldn't repair the garden just yet. I'd like to take a look at that camera footage."

"This way." Bella led the way into her office and pulled up the recording.

The deputy watched for a while. "Definitely looks like a teen." He sighed. "Without a good look at his face…" he leaned closer to the screen. "I recognize his shoes, I think." He took a still photo of the perpetrator, then made it larger. "See? I know the young man who draws on the white soles of his shoes."

The doorbell rang.

"I'll get it." Deacon went to answer the door. He opened it to see a young man holding a yearbook. Deacon's gaze fell to the boy's shoes. The very shoes spotted in the video. He reached out and yanked the boy inside.

Chapter Ten

"I, uh, brought the yearbook you asked for." A pale, frightened boy entered Bella's office, Deacon right behind him.

"Thank you." She took the book. "What's wrong?"

"Look at his shoes," Deacon growled.

Her gaze dropped. "You tore up my garden?"

The boy shrank back, then jumped forward when he bumped against Deacon. His gaze flicked to the deputy who had stood from the chair. "I, uh…" His shoulders slumped. "Someone paid me."

"How did you keep my dog from barking?" Bella crossed her arms.

"I gave it a bone from the steak I had for supper last night." He hung his head.

"Who paid you?" Deputy Hudson pushed the boy into the chair. "Because you should know better, Ryan Jones. Your father is going to tan your hide."

"I don't know who he is. Some rich dude who paid me a hundred bucks. That's a lot of money."

"I hope you didn't spend it yet because you're going to need it to pay your fine for vandalism." The deputy pulled a cell phone from his pocket. "I'm calling your father to meet us at the sheriff's office." He placed the call, then took the young man to his squad car.

"At least that mystery is solved. Let's take this book to the kitchen. I'll make coffee." Bella set the yearbook on the island. "Do you think the Jones boy will have to pay restitution? It would help repair the garden." She glanced out the window where Rufus knelt in the dirt trying to salvage what he could of the rose bushes that had grown there for as long as Bella could remember.

The sight broke her heart every time she looked outside.

Deacon gave her a one-armed hug. "It'll be okay."

One arm wasn't enough. She turned and wrapped both arms around his waist, resting her cheek on his broad chest. "I know. Thank you for being here. I'm not sure I could do this alone."

His hold tightened. "Bella, you're a strong woman, just like Mildred. You'd get through this without me."

They stood that way for several minutes before Bella pulled back. "I'm sorry. That was forward of me, but I just needed a hug."

He grinned. "I'm happy to hug you anytime you want."

Her face heated. She cleared her throat and moved to make the coffee before she embarrassed herself further. Behind her came the rustling of pages being turned.

"Found Emily's photo."

Bella carried two cups of coffee to the island, setting one next to Deacon and carrying the other to the stool next to him. She glanced at the page where he pointed. A pretty girl with long dark hair and light-colored eyes stared up in black and white. A coy smile graced her lips. "I can see how she turned heads."

"Luckily this town wasn't very big back then. None of the high school classes were more than ninety students. Let's start writing these names down and see which ones are still around."

She slid off the stool and fetched paper and a pen. "Read them off to me. Let's start with just her class."

When he'd finished, she tore the paper in half. "Did you bring a laptop with you?"

"Sure did." He left the room, returning a moment later with his device.

The two of them searched the internet for any class members from Emily's graduating class who were still alive. When they'd finished, they had five names of classmates still living in Misty Hollow. Linda Marie Johnson, Sylvia Ann Walker, Charles Edward Harrison, John William Thompson, and Henry Davidson whom they'd already talked to. "Robert Raney must be older or younger." Bella flipped back through the yearbook, not finding his name. No matter. They knew where he was.

"If you don't mind making the calls, see who is willing to talk to us, I want to head to the barn and make sure Keith is taking proper care of the horses. He came highly recommended, but I'd still like to check." Deacon stood.

"Sure. I'll let you know what I find out." She dialed the first number, thankful for the ability to find anything on the internet with a little effort.

"Good afternoon. My name is Isabella Harper, granddaughter of Mildred Harper. I'd like to speak to Linda Marie Johnson, please."

The woman on the other end laughed. "I'm Fuller now, but yes, that would be me. How is Mildred?"

"She passed a few months ago."

"I'm sorry to hear that. She was such a lovely woman."

"Thank you." Bella smiled. "I'm actually calling about a party that happened in the 1970s. A party that might've resulted in the death of Emily Marks."

"I wouldn't know anything about that. My parents didn't allow me to go to parties, much less ones at the lake." The woman's warm tone had chilled. "I really can't help you." She hung up.

Bella received the same response from the three other names she called. With a sigh, she dialed the last number and repeated her spiel to a woman once named Sylvia Ann Walker.

"Of course, I knew Mildred. We were best friends. I'm afraid I'm not comfortable answering any questions over the phone."

"I'm willing to meet you somewhere." Bella held her breath, hoping the woman would say yes.

"Meet me at the library in half an hour. Six o'clock. Those responsible for Emily's death would never set foot in a library. You'll recognize me by my red hat. I belong to the local Red Hat Society." She chuckled.

"I'll be there." Bella hung up and raced off to find Deacon.

They arrived at the library with two minutes to spare. Bella led the way up and down the library aisles until she spotted a woman in her sixties wearing a red hat at a table in a far corner. "Mrs. Walker?"

"It's Bishop now. You can call me Sylvia." She

smiled and invited them to sit across from her. Wrinkles lined her face, but her eyes were sharp. The woman removed her red hat and placed it on the table in front of her. "Before you ask your questions, may I ask why you're interested in something that happened so long ago?"

"We found some letters written to my grandmother from a man named Albert telling her about the night Emily died. A night full of secrets."

Deacon took Bella's hand in his under the table. "There have been some incidents at the inn that appear as if someone wants Bella to stop searching for answers."

Bella nodded. "We're especially interested in what might have occurred between Henry Davidson and Robert Raney Sr." Bella's hand warmed in Deacon's. "You said you were best friends with my grandmother, but she never mentioned you."

Sylvia shrugged. "We were like sisters at one point, but...powerful people have a way of pulling other people apart."

"What do you mean?" Bella leaned forward.

"Years ago, Misty Hollow was the target of a real estate scheme. Something that also happens now from time to time. Over the years, the Willow Ridge Inn has been the jewel some ruthless people want to grab. Mildred and I actually ran off a developer once."

"I've had the same type of run-in with a man named Garrett Boyd."

"Ah. Following in his father's footsteps, I see."

"What does any of this have to do with Emily Marks?" Deacon interrupted.

"Poor Emily was the one feeding me and Mildred

information, you see." Sylvia fiddled with the rim of her hat. "She came from an abusive home and would have done anything to escape it, even try to get pregnant by one of the boys from wealthy families."

"Davidson and Raney." Bella glanced at Deacon.

"Yes. They'd often talk about what their fathers were up to. Emily would then tell me and Mildred. We were probably the only girls in our class who didn't shun her. Anyway, when she died, Mildred and I figured she'd been killed to shut her up, but we couldn't prove any of it. My father found out what we were up to and forbade me to have anything to do with Mildred after that. He was afraid I'd meet the same fate as Emily."

Bella shook her head. "Such a shame. My grandmother never stopped trying to find out what happened. Especially after the letters she received from Albert." Sadness filled Bella at the tragic loss of life.

Sylvia nodded. "They'll do whatever it takes to protect their interests." She reached across the table and took Bella's free hand. "Be careful, dear. If you keep digging, they'll come after you in a big way."

The warning punched Bella in the gut. "What about you? You'll be a target now for speaking to us."

"I'm leaving tonight to visit my sister. Don't you worry about me. I'll be just fine." She stood and put her hat back on her head. "I'll come back when this is all over."

Bella got to her feet, slipping her hand from Deacon's. "I won't let them win. No matter what it takes, I'll find out the truth."

Sylvia's eyes softened. "You're as brave as Mildred. Just be careful. Those men have stolen enough. Don't let them take anything else." She turned to Deacon. "Keep her safe, young man."

"I plan to."

A steely resolve filled Bella. Her grandmother's fight wasn't over. Bella would exact justice for her murder and for Emily's. Grandma had faced the force that drove Boyd and the two men who were responsible for Emily's death all those years ago. The obstacle facing Bella now was how to confront Raney.

With Davidson in the nursing home, the only one who could tell them what really happened that night was Raney. "We need to visit Davidson again. Although we managed to get a bit of information from him, maybe we can persuade him to turn on Raney."

"That's not a bad idea." Deacon's hand warmed the small of her back as he led her to his truck. "The building for venues should be finished tomorrow. We can head out once you've finalized things with the construction crew."

"Awesome. I can start decorating." She grinned. "I can't wait to start generating income."

"When does the first paying guest arrive?"

"Tomorrow morning." The next day promised to be a busy one.

Deacon glanced at his phone as he slid into the truck. "Boyd's been arrested. Hopefully, you won't have to deal with him anymore."

"One down, two more to go." She clicked her seatbelt into place. Maybe the end was in sight after all.

Her throat clogged, and she started coughing. "You okay?" Concern spread across his face.

"Yes, I just have a big lump in my throat. If I hadn't suspected something off about my grandmother's death, those men might never have been caught."

"They aren't caught yet."

"No, but they will be. I promise you that." Even if she suffered the same fate as her grandmother and Emily, enough questions had been raised with the sheriff that she felt confident he'd continue investigating.

"This will be very dangerous."

"I know." She gave a shaky smile. "You don't have to go any further with me."

"If you think I'll let you go this alone, you're nuts." He started the truck. "I'm here for as long as you need me."

For that she'd be eternally grateful.

Chapter Eleven

The next morning, Bella and Deacon once again sat across from Davidson. The man seemed more alert and belligerent than the last time they'd spoken to him.

"I told you I've got nothing to say." He glowered and crossed his arms.

Bella leaned forward. "That isn't what Raney says." She'd chosen to go ahead with the tactic of making the man believe his friend was spilling the beans.

"What's he saying?" Davidson's face darkened.

"That you're responsible for Emily's death. That you didn't like a girl like her trying to worm her way into your family." Bella shrugged. "So…you got rid of her."

"That's a lie. The girl had loose lips, spreading news she had no business spreading." His eyes widened as if he knew he'd said too much.

"Was she pregnant, Mr. Davidson?" Bella needed to get hold of the autopsy report from all those years ago.

"Who knows?" The convulsing of his throat as he

tried to swallow told the opposite.

"Was it yours or Raney's?" She pressed the issue.

"Like I said, who knows?" He glanced toward one of the aides, his eyes pleading for help.

"Before you're taken back to your room," Deacon said. "Let me tell you that the truth will come out. We know that you know and even had a hand in what happened to Emily Marks. Same with Mildred Harper. When was the last time Raney came to visit you?"

Bella's eyes widened. She hadn't thought to look at the visitor roster.

"He comes twice a week." Davidson hitched his chin. "We're still best friends, and we still co-own a business. Of course, he comes to visit." His eyes started to glaze over, and he began to mumble.

They'd lost him. Bella stood. "Thank you for your time, Mr. Davidson." She leaned close to whisper. "If you'd confess, maybe the guilt wouldn't be sending you into dementia quite so fast." She glanced at the clock on the wall. Time to return to the inn before her paying guest arrived.

When they entered the kitchen, Ida alerted them to the fact that the guest was running late and wouldn't arrive until the next morning. "Their room's all ready to go."

"Thank you." While Deacon headed upstairs to his room, Bella exited through the back door and made her way to the newly repaired barn. A fresh coat of red paint, some planters waiting to be filled outside the door, and a freshly laid pebble path welcomed anyone who wanted to rent the venue.

Pride filled her. She'd accomplished so much in the month since she'd returned to Misty Hollow.

Grandma would be proud. She spent the rest of the day planting flowers around the barn and decorating the inside, then snapped photos and worked on marketing. Deacon said he needed to return to the ranch for a few hours to help find a lost calf.

When Deacon hadn't arrived by nine p.m., she went to bed. Ghost jumped up beside her, and within minutes she fell asleep.

Something shattered downstairs. Bella bolted upright. Ghost growled deep in his throat. Could Deacon have knocked something over when he came home? She glanced at the clock on her nightstand. Just past midnight.

Another crash followed, the unmistakable sound of glass breaking, followed by heavy footsteps. Someone was inside the inn.

She grabbed her phone from beside the bed. "Come, Ghost. Stay by my side."

The dog padded beside her as she crept down the stairs. She peered into the office. Papers flew. A man tossed furniture, then rifled through her desk.

Ghost barked. Bella grabbed his collar to keep him from attacking.

The man whirled, clutching a knife. "Where are they?"

"Where is what?" Her stomach dropped, and her gaze locked on the weapon in his hand.

"The letters." His lip curled. "The ones old man Albert sent."

"Who are you?"

"Answer the question!"

"I don't have any letters." She fought to keep her gaze from flicking to the window. Where were Ida and

Rufus? Deacon? Someone had to hear the noise besides her.

The man advanced.

Ghost strained against Bella's hold.

"I will find them, Miss Harper." His eyes glittered from under the ski mask he wore. "Things will go easier for you if you hand them over."

"No." She backed up.

"I'm not here alone. My partner is searching outside. We will find them." He pulled her grandmother's journal from under his jacket, then leaped through the broken window.

Bella's gaze fell on the rolltop desk. He'd found the secret drawer. Her grandmother's notes were gone.

She fell to her knees among the wreckage of her office, letting go of Ghost's collar. In a single bound, her dog leaped through the shattered window after the thief.

~

It had taken way too long to find the missing calf, which had managed to get itself tangled in a thick briar patch. Deacon's hands showed the proof of the night's work.

Exhaustion coated his limbs as he climbed from his truck. A fierce barking drew his attention to the paddock in time to see Ghost streaking after a man who jumped onto a four-wheeler, then sped off into the night. Seconds later, another one followed the first.

Deacon raced for the house. "Bella!" He found her on her knees in the office. His gaze scanned the wrecked office before returning to her. "Are you okay?"

"Guess so. A man broke in. He took my

grandmother's journal. The letters!" She jumped to her feet and sprinted outside to where she'd buried the letters.

Nothing under the spigot but a gaping hole.

"They took the letters." Her voice shook. "They now know what we know."

"Thankfully, the sheriff has a copy of them."

Her eyes glittered in the moonlight as she glanced up at him. "I think they did something to Ida and Rufus. They should've heard the commotion. Where's Ghost?"

"He took off after the four-wheelers."

She clutched his shirt. "We have to go after him. What if they hurt him?"

"People first, sweetheart." The dog would have to fend for itself until they located Ida and Rufus.

After searching every room, Deacon suggested the hidden passages. They found Ida and Rufus gagged and tied behind the living room wall.

Deacon removed their gags, then cut through the zip ties binding their hands. "What happened?"

"A man came to my room." Ida struggled to her feet. "Brandished a knife at me and told me to go with him, or he'd gut me like a fish." She shrugged. "So, I went with him. I'm no fool."

"Pretty much the same scenario for me," Rufus said rubbing his wrists. "Everyone all right?"

"They ransacked my office, but other than that, yes. Let's go find Ghost." Bella tugged at Deacon's arm.

"Okay. Ida, do you mind having a pot of coffee ready when we return and calling the sheriff's department?"

"We'll take care of that." Rufus nodded. "Go find

the dog. Keith is most likely sleeping with headphones on. Told me he liked to sleep to music."

"We'll check on him on the way to the field behind the inn." Deacon grabbed a flashlight from the kitchen, then headed outdoors. Sure enough, the young man slept, headphones on, oblivious to the night's events. Deacon let him sleep. The guy would find out later.

An early morning mist hovered over the lake and pastureland, lending an eerie effect. Clouds scouted across the moon, offering little light. They stopped at the edge of the lake and listened.

The far off drone of engines told him the two intruders were gone. Knowing Mildred had been murdered and how close those men had come to harming Bella clutched his heart with an icy grip. The next time he got called to the ranch, he'd make sure to find someone to watch the house.

"Ghost!" Bella's voice echoed across the lake. "Here, boy." She gasped as the dog emerged from the dark forest. "He's okay."

She ran toward the dog and the dog toward her as two lovers in a sappy chick flick. Deacon couldn't help but wonder if she'd react the same if he went missing and was found. He also wondered why he cared. Deacon was helping her find Mildred's killer because he'd cared for Bella's grandmother. He hadn't expected to get involved in an almost fifty-year murder, too.

Back at the inn, they got to work setting the office to rights. Bella set aside anything the thief had missed that pertained to the murders.

"At least we aren't starting from scratch." She sighed. "You're right. We did give copies of everything to the sheriff. Surely, the thieves would know that. We aren't set back that much in our quest for justice."

Deacon's admiration for her grew. "You're incredible. After all this, you're still ready to fight."

Bella blew out a slow breath. "They're trying to scare me into giving up. That won't work with me. It only makes me more determined."

"Agreed. We have to be more careful, though. Tonight could've ended so much worse."

"Yes, Ghost could've been killed or injured."

A laugh escaped him. "I'm talking about you, Bella."

She grinned. "Guess I care about my dog more than I do myself."

"That's obvious."

When they'd finished putting the office to rights, they headed for the kitchen and coffee as the sun peeked over the mountain. "I've eggs and bacon almost ready," Ida said. "Thought you might be hungry."

Bella glanced around. "Where's Rufus?"

"Went back to bed for an hour or so. I'll do the same once I'm finished here."

Deacon took the spatula from her. "Go ahead. I know my way around eggs and bacon. We'll clean up after ourselves."

"You're a good man, Deacon Simpson." She patted his cheek, then hung up her apron. "See you in a bit."

"You should get some sleep after breakfast." Deacon shot Bella a look.

"I can't. Our guest is arriving around nine." She glanced at the clock. "That's only four hours away."

"You could sleep for three and be fine. Ida has the room all ready." He scooped eggs and bacon onto a plate and handed it to her as the doorbell rang. "That would be the sheriff's department. I'll get it."

He opened the door to a man in a deputy uniform he didn't know.

"I'm Deputy Bolton." The man smiled. "Being the new guy, they sent me to see about a break-in."

"It took you so long we've already cleaned up." Bella glared over a slice of bacon. "Coffee?" Bolton shrugged. "Just show me where the damage is. We're pretty busy over at the station, which is why I was hired."

Bella led the way. "A few things are broken, but I've put most things back where they belong."

"The perp came through the window?"

"Yes."

The deputy circled the room picking up items, then setting them back down. He opened the antique rolltop desk, ran his fingers over the keyboard to Bella's laptop, then faced her and Deacon. "Anything else?"

Something seemed off about the man. "They dug a hole out back," Deacon said. "Care to see?"

"Does it have anything to do with what's missing?"

"Yes, Officer, it does." Deacon crossed his arms. "I'm wondering why you didn't show your ID when I answered the door and why you haven't asked what's missing?"

"My mistake." He grinned and flashed his badge. "Thought you'd know who I was by the uniform. As to what's missing, the person who called said there was a break-in and some files were taken. Is that wrong?"

"No." Deacon kept his eyes trained on the deputy. The man's smile seemed too bright. "Mind if I ask about Garrett Boyd?"

"I don't care. The man posted bail."

The doorbell rang. Deacon opened the door to see a man in a dark suit, briefcase in one hand and a suitcase in the other.

Chapter Twelve

"I'm Thomas Wells." The man thrust out his hand. "I'll be staying here at the inn for a few days."

"Welcome to Willow Ridge." Bella had followed Deacon from her office, the deputy right behind her.

Ghost growled.

The man's gaze flickered. "Will he bite?"

"Only if you try to harm me." Bella smiled. "Please, let me show you to your room. What brings you to Misty Hollow?"

"I'm a bit of a history buff, and I'm intrigued with the rich history of these mountains." He glanced around the room she led him to and nodded. "This will do nicely. Thank you."

"Breakfast is at seven, supper at five. You're on your own for lunch, but I'm sure our cook, Ida, will fix you something if you ask. Don't hesitate to find me if you need anything."

She hastened out of the room, her heart warm. The inn's first guest since she'd taken over! The joy dispelled some of the gloom of the theft.

By the time she returned downstairs, the deputy had left. Deacon stood on the porch watching him leave. "I don't like that man," he said.

"He didn't seem too concerned about the break-in." She faced him. "I'd like to go into town and question a few more of the old-timers. We need more information to take to the sheriff in order to bring Raney down."

She turned to go back into the house when she bumped into Thomas who stood in the doorway. "Did you need something?"

"No, just looking around. Pictures didn't do justice to the beauty of this place." He stepped aside so she could enter.

"Thank you." She collected her purse and cell phone from her bedroom, then pulled the door closed behind her before joining Deacon outside. "Any idea where to start?"

"Are you hungry?" He arched a brow.

"Not really, and I have too many things going on."

"Then the diner?" He grinned, obviously ignoring her answer.

"The diner it is." The man was always hungry.

They were lucky enough to get the last booth by the hallway to the restrooms. "Is it always this crowded?"

"Yep. This place has the best biscuits and gravy, whether it's white or chocolate. Me, though...I'm going with the steak and eggs."

She widened her eyes. "That's a lot of food."

"I'm a big man." He grinned.

That he was. A few inches over six feet, broad shoulders, toned...he could easily grace the cover of any western magazine. She focused on the menu in front of her when he caught her staring. "I'm going with biscuits and chocolate gravy. I'm nowhere near as big as you."

"No, darlin', you aren't. A stiff wind would blow you away." He winked.

What was going on? Was he flirting with her?

The diner door opened, drawing her attention that way as Mayor Raney walked in. He frowned at the lack of seating. Within seconds, two men scooted from their booth and offered the table to him, taking their plates to the counter.

Hmm. Raney hadn't said a word, yet those men willingly gave up their seats. Before she could turn her attention back to Deacon, Wells entered and strode to where Raney sat.

She held the menu in front of her face. "Wells just joined Raney."

Deacon started to turn.

"Don't look! He can't see you from where you sit. Hopefully, he won't notice me. He said he was here for history, so why meet with the mayor?"

"To ask historical questions?" Deacon shrugged. "It does seem suspicious. I got the impression he didn't know anyone here. Keep an eye on them."

It could be that the man wanted to question the mayor about Misty Hollow and the surrounding area, but Bella's gut told her it was more than that. Wells narrowed his eyes in her direction, then quickly smiled and waved.

Raney followed his gaze, frowned in Bella's direction, then turned back to Wells. A minute later, the two left the diner without ordering. Very suspicious.

She leaned toward Deacon. "Is there someone here we can question?"

An elderly man in faded coveralls came down the

hall from the men's room. Deacon waved him over. "Bella, meet Wilbur Stillwell. Wilbur, Isabella Harper, Mildred's granddaughter." Deacon motioned to the seat next to him and scooted over.

"Ah, the granddaughter of the love that got away." He sat. "What a hard deal this town received when Mildred died."

"I believe someone murdered her." Bella tilted her head.

"Some do believe that, yes." He waved to the waitress. "Coffee along with the special, Ma'am. It's always better to eat with someone rather than alone at the counter."

Deacon laughed. "You're always talking to someone at the counter. At lease whenever I'm in here."

"You got me there." He folded his hands on the table. "I know you didn't invite me to join you unless you had something to ask me."

"That isn't the only reason, Mr. Stillwell." Bella hated for him to think them rude.

"Of course, it is. Ask away. I'd do anything for Mildred."

Bella took a deep breath. "Are you familiar with the events on the night Emily Marks died in 1976?"

Deacon shot her a sharp look. "You found out the year?"

"The yearbook." She smiled. "That's the year Emily was a senior. Is that the year she died, Mr. Stillwell?"

He nodded. "Call me Wilbur. I wasn't at that party, if that's what you're asking. I'd graduated three years before and worked the farm with my dad. No time for such foolishness. But, I did hear the stories." He lowered his voice. "The Raneys have been here a long time, ma'am. They have lot of friends. Some folks won't like you asking questions."

"I intend to find out the truth, Wilbur, especially if my grandmother was killed because of what happened to Emily."

"There's truth in that. Mildred didn't go to that party either, but she was Emily's friend." He straightened as the server brought their meals. When the girl left, he continued. "Emily had dated Davidson for a while and moved on to Raney. Poor girl would do almost anything to leave home. Her daddy beat her and her mother something awful." He popped a piece of bacon into his mouth.

"Why was she killed?" Bella was growing tired of the runaround. Get to the point already.

"Because she told Mildred and Sylvia how the two boys' families were cheating folks out of their land." He dropped his fork onto his plate with a clatter. "Calling in bank loans. Davidson's father owned the bank, offering pennies on the dollar for each acre…the dirtiest pillow talk, if you ask me. Emily violated those boys' trust and paid for it."

"Do you have proof?" Bella's heart raced.

He shook his head. "I'm guessing your grandmother must've dug something up."

"I found letters to her from Albert."

"You find out all that man knew, and you'll have your proof."

"He's dead."

"His house still stands in a holler on the mountain." He gave them directions. "I'm guessing anything he knew might be buried up there." He wiped his mouth with his napkin and slid from the booth. "Y'all be careful. Those men aren't to be trifled with." He started to pull some money from his pocket only to have Deacon still his hand.

"Your breakfast is on me."

"Mighty obliged." He nodded and left the diner.

Bella clamped her hands together before taking a bit of her now cold chocolate gravy. "He told us more than anyone. We've got some digging to do."

~

As Deacon drove out of town, he glanced in his rearview mirror. Raney and Thomas Wells stepped from the mayor's office. Raney's glare followed them down the street. Deacon's suspicion about the man grew. Thomas Wells wasn't in town to dig up history unless that history was what happened to Emily Marks. "Let's pick up Ghost before heading to Albert's hollow. No one will be able to sneak up on us with him around."

They retrieved the dog and drove the twenty minutes to where an old log cabin stood surrounded by weeds. Plywood had been nailed over the windows, now rotting and pulling away. No one had been there in a very long time.

He shoved his door open and stepped into knee-high grass and weeds. "It should be too cold for snakes, but be careful anyway."

"Snakes?" Bella paled.

"They're more scared of you." He grinned.

"Yeah, right." She studied the ground around her. "Where do we start looking?"

"The house." He headed to the porch. His booted

foot went through the top step. He pulled it free and turned the doorknob. The door opened easily to reveal a dust-filled room with sheet-covered furniture as if someone had intended to return. Had Albert passed before he could return to his family home?

Deacon's feet stirred up dust. Bella sneezed behind him. "I'll check the bedrooms if you want to search the front rooms."

"Okay."

While she moved to the kitchen, he headed for the back of two bedrooms. A third bedroom had been converted to an office with a sleeper sofa. He turned into that one instead, figuring any important papers might be stashed there. Although, that seemed obvious to him.

After searching the closet, the desk drawers, and under the bed, he found nothing. He moved to the window. At the edge of the clearing, he spotted a treehouse built in a large oak.

"Bella, follow me." He'd once hidden everything he cherished in the treehouse his father had built him.

With Bella and Ghost following, he trudged through the weeds to the oak. Wood planks, most of them missing, were nailed into the tree trunk. He didn't trust them to hold his weight. Instead, he jumped, grabbing hold of the lowest branch and swinging himself up.

Could there be something up here? It seemed too easy, but then all the focus had been on what Mildred knew, not what Albert knew.

An old steamer trunk rested in a corner of the tiny tree house. Excitement beat in Deacon's chest as he wiped away the dust and opened the lid.

Inside, under worn comic books and baseball cards sat a cigar box covered with painted pasta. Holding his breath, Deacon opened the box. Inside were several pages of details regarding the infamous party in 1976. Good man, Albert. Deacon tucked the pages into his shirt and returned the cigar box to the chest.

"Find anything?" Bella called up.

"Sure did." He swung down, landing with a thud in front of her. "Let's get out of here." He took her hand and headed toward the truck.

Ghost, fur bristling, blocked their way.

"Someone is out there," Bella whispered. "Quiet, Ghost. He doesn't act this way about an animal."

"Get down." Deacon pulled her into the weeds. "Stay low. We need to get to the truck."

"You think someone followed us?"

"Yep." Staying as low as possible, he kept a tight grip on her hand and pulled her toward the truck.

A yelp escaped her as a shot rang out. They were going to have to make a run for it. "Stay with me and stay low."

Another shot sent them sprinting. Deacon pressed them against the opposite side of the truck and opened the passenger-side door. "Once I'm in, you and Ghost get in as fast as you can and hunker down."

She nodded, her eyes wide.

He crawled to the driver's side and turned the key in the ignition as Ghost bounded in, then Bella. She slammed the door behind her and wrapped her arms around the dog's neck.

Deacon pressed the gas pedal to the floor and spun dirt as he sped away from the cabin.

A bullet shattered the back window, peppering

them with glass. His cheek burned from where he'd been cut. Staying as low over the steering wheel as possible and still see out the window, he veered onto the main road and out of gunshot range.

Chapter Thirteen

Deacon drove straight to the sheriff's office. Bella put a restraining hand on his arm. "Let's look at what you found before we turn it over."

"Okay." He glanced in the rearview mirror, then pulled several sheets of wrinkled papers from inside his shirt. "Can you hand me the napkins in the glove box?"

Bella grabbed a handful and waited while he dabbed at the cuts on his face. "Do they hurt?"

"They sting a little, but I'll live. Are you cut?"

"No. I'm sure my hair is full of glass though. I'll worry about that when we get out of the truck." She started reading. "Albert says here that Emily was found strangled to death by the lake. He again lists Davidson and Raney as the primary suspects, although the local authorities at the time blamed her death on a vagrant. He says an innocent man went to jail." She scanned the pages. "Albert dug into town records, property deeds, and police reports. Deacon, everything we need to stop these men is right here in our hands." Her heart beat faster as she read.

"Albert named a witness to Emily's murder. A young woman named Annie who vanished shortly thereafter. No one ever found out what happened to her. This is worse than we thought." She took photos of each page, then shoved them into her purse. "I don't want these in our possession any longer than necessary."

"I agree." He shoved his door open. "Whoever shot at us will be coming for whatever we found. We need something to give them when they do."

"I'll make up some dummy reports, using only minor details when we return to the inn." She practically ran into the sheriff's station, bypassed the wide-eyed receptionist, and barged into the man's office.

A very pretty woman with ebony hair and a haunted look in her hazel eyes whirled to face the door, her hand reaching for the gun at her hip.

"It's fine, Shea. This is Isabella Harper and Deacon Simpson." Sheriff Westbrook frowned. "This is Shea Callahan. What happened to the two of you?"

Bella thrust the papers at him while Deacon filled him in on where he'd found them and being shot at. When he'd finished, Bella fell into a chair. "We need protection."

The sheriff exhaled heavily. "Shea, how about you take over here a little later than planned and watch over these two who insist on doing my job?"

"You're the new sheriff?" Bella asked.

"Is that a problem?" The woman's eyes narrowed.

"No, but you're…so pretty."

The new sheriff bit her lip to keep from smiling.

"She's very capable, Miss Harper, I assure you." Sheriff Westbrook flipped through the papers Bella had handed them. "If you read the newspapers, you'll know that."

"I heard about the incident on the mountain," Deacon said. "I actually expected you to look more…manly."

"I'm not sure whether that's a compliment or not." She turned to Sheriff Westbrook. "Sure, I'll see what I can do. First, I need to find a place to stay until I buy a house."

"I own The Willow Ridge Inn. You can have a room for free as long as you need it." Relief at having law enforcement staying under her roof eased some of the tension in her shoulders. She rattled off the address and stood. "Welcome to Misty Hollow, Sheriff Callahan."

"I have a German shepherd."

"That's fine." Bella smiled. "My dog won't mind."

"Before you go, Shea, let me make you a copy of these pages." Sheriff Westbrook headed to a small copier in the corner of his office.

"Email them to me, Sheriff. I don't want hard copies." With a nod and a promise to see them later, Sheriff Callahan left the office.

Sheriff Westbrook nodded, then turned to Bella and Deacon. "Make sure you don't run her off. I'm ready to retire."

Deacon laughed. "We'll do our best. Thank you. I feel a lot better knowing Bella's survival doesn't rely solely on me."

"I'm doing a pretty good job of taking care of myself, you know." Bella glared as they returned to the truck. "I'm not a helpless, fragile little girl."

"I know that. You're one of the strongest women I know." He smiled over the top of the truck. "Let's head to the mechanics and see about getting my back window replaced."

"Tell me about Sheriff Callahan." She climbed into the truck.

"You'd get more info by looking her up on the internet. She's one tough lady, that's for sure." He pulled out of the parking lot and headed east.

Bella read about the new sheriff's fight on the mountain during a weekend away with her college friends. The article mentioned hand-to-hand fighting, being hunted through the woods, and her killing some of those who terrorized them. "She's going to be a great protector. Wow."

"She ran for sheriff unopposed based solely on Westbrook's word. This town is lucky to have her." Deacon pulled in front of the mechanic garage.

A man in greasy coveralls ambled toward them. "Hey, Deacon." His gaze ran over the truck. "Need a new window, I see. Let me check to see whether I have one for your model." He sauntered back into the garage. When he returned, he told them he'd have to pick up a windshield from Langley and would be by when the garage closed to replace the window. "I'll be at the inn before dark."

As soon as they returned to the inn, Bella let Ida know to prepare a room for the new sheriff. "I'm not sure how long she'll be staying with us. How is our other guest?"

"He's gone a lot." Ida shrugged. "Flits in and out of here without saying a word. Not that I care. His business is his own, but he isn't what I'd call friendly."

As long as he paid for his room, Bella didn't care how often the man was gone.

~

Deacon jerked toward the front door as someone leaned on the doorbell. "I'll get it." He motioned for Bella to stay with Ida. As usual, she didn't listen.

After peering through the peephole and seeing Boyd, he yanked the door open. "What do you want?"

"Let me in." The man pushed past him. "I need to speak with the two of you." He headed for the living room.

Deacon raised his eyebrows at Bella, then followed the man. He crossed his arms. "Talk."

"If you're here to pressure me into selling, you can leave." Bella jerked her head toward the door.

"Not this time." Boyd rubbed his hands down his face. "This time I'm here to warn you. The two of you have no idea what you're dealing with. You've got to stop nosing around and asking questions. People aren't happy about your visits to the nursing home to see Davidson."

"What people?" Deacon demanded.

"Just people. Important, powerful people." He sat on the sofa. "Emily Marks's death is only a piece of a sprawling network of illicit activities. She stuck her nose where it didn't belong, and look where it got her."

"Why are you telling us this?" Deacon dropped into the chair across from him. Bella perched on the armrest.

"Because you won't sell, Miss Harper, those very same people are unhappy with me. I'll be leaving town as soon as I can and wanted to give you this one last warning. I was purchasing the inn for...Well, telling you his name will get me killed. Just suffice it to say that the properties I purchase are used to "clean" funds from dubious enterprises. A resort is perfect for such things."

"You're talking about money laundering." Bella gasped. "It's been going on since the 70s?"

"Way before then." He shook his head. "You're playing with fire. Both of you."

Deacon locked gazes with the man. "Why not go to the sheriff?"

"That would definitely get me killed." Boyd stood. He glanced out the window. His eyes widened. "Time to go. I'll leave out the back. Heed my words. Somewhere in the hidden places of this house is all the proof you need." With another panicked look at the window, he darted out the kitchen door.

Deacon moved to the window in time to see the inn's guest get out of his car. Why would Boyd be frightened of this man?

Thomas Wells pulled a briefcase from his backseat, then strolled to the front door of the inn. He cast a questioning look at Deacon and Bella, then proceeded up the stairs without a word.

"Where's Boyd's car?" Bella asked, joining Deacon at the window. "Unless he expected Wells to arrive, he'd have parked in front of the inn."

"The man does rent a room from you. Boyd was simply being cautious." He faced her. "I thought we'd searched all the secret places of this house."

"Guess we'll start over and try to be more thorough. If Boyd is right, we'll find what we need to end this. Then, you'll be free to return to the ranch."

His heart skipped a beat. Returning to the ranch meant not seeing Bella every day and spending almost every minute of those days with her. Returning to his previous life didn't seem as sweet as it had before meeting her.

"What?" She raised her lovely face to his.

"Nothing." He cleared his throat of the lump that had formed there. "You're right. It's time to put an end to this danger."

A puzzled expression flickered in her amazing blue eyes. "You look sad all of a sudden."

He forced a smile. "Just tired, I guess. It's been a busy few days."

"We need to have some fun. How about a horseback ride? It's been ages since I've ridden."

"That sounds like a wonderful idea. Meet me in the barn in fifteen minutes."

Her gaze returned to the window. "Sheriff Callahan is here. I'll be there once she's settled."

Twenty minutes later, Bella joined him along with Ghost, the new sheriff, and Heidi, her German shepherd.

"I'll saddle another horse." So much for a ride with just him and Bella.

"Sorry to intrude, but I am here to provide protection." A subtle smile graced the sheriff's face. "Call me Shea. I don't want to advertise who I am." She ran her hand down one of the horse's muzzle. "I'm looking for property to buy where I can have a horse. If you hear of such a place, please let me know. Also, a recommendation of a good horse seller would be nice."

"The Rocking W Ranch is the best place to purchase a horse." Deacon led a mare from a stall and proceeded to saddle her. "As for property, check with Lucy at the diner. She knows everything about everything in Misty Hollow." Except for whoever killed

Emily Marks and Mildred Harper.

Once he'd saddled the horses, he helped Bella onto hers, then led the way toward a riding path he knew behind the inn. The sheriff was kind enough to hang back a bit. The dogs, noses to the ground, ran ahead.

"I get the impression you wanted it to be just the two of us on this ride." Bella tilted her head.

"Would that be bad?"

She bit her bottom lip, a gesture that did funny things to his stomach. "No, it would be nice."

In a moment of bravery, he blurted out, "Maybe you'll let me take you on a real date when this is all over."

"Maybe." Her cheeks turned a delightful shade of pink.

He grinned like a goon. "Race you to the creek?"

"I don't know where the creek is." She laughed and clicked her tongue to her horse who took off like a rocket.

"You, Isabella Harper, are a little liar." Laughing, he rode after her.

Chapter Fourteen

The inn seemed to hold its breath as Bella, Deacon, and Shea stepped into the passageway off the kitchen pantry. The worn wooden floor muffled their footsteps.

"Search the walls for a secret door we missed the last time." Deacon shined his flashlight in front of them. "I took another look at the blueprint last night, and there's another room off this passageway."

Bella ran her hand over the rough walls pressing at different intervals in the hopes something would click.

"Here." Shea's voice barely rose above a whisper.

Bella turned to see a narrow door swing open. She stepped inside to see a cracked armoire taking up most of the space. It creaked as she opened it.

Inside sat a stack of yellowed newspapers and grainy photographs that told of a long-buried scandal. A chill ran down her spine. The photos revealed a party with familiar faces from 1976.

Emily, young, vibrant, and pretty, stood between younger versions of Davidson and Raney. Each of them smiled and raised a toast with a drink in their hands. Another photo showed an unsmiling Mildred and

Sylvia sitting near the edge of the lake. A third picture showed her grandmother's cheery smile. Oh, how Bella missed that smile.

"Take a look at these." Deacon pulled some papers from inside a newspaper. "These contain information about detailed real estate deals, shady bank transactions, and more mentions of Davidson and Raney's fathers."

"That's the proof we need." Bella peered over his shoulder.

"I'm going to go stand guard," Shea said. "Gather up what evidence you can and join me in the living room. We need to get those things to Sheriff Westbrook." She hurried back the way they came.

Bella returned her attention to the photographs. A candid shot revealed Emily trying to pull away from Davidson's grip while Raney laughed in the background. Another showed her struggling as Davidson held her to the ground and lay on top of her trying to kiss her. These photos appeared to be taken away from the rest of the partygoers.

"Deacon, Emily might have been raped by Davidson and Raney before they killed her." Tears clogged her throat.

"Here's a diary. I think it's Emily's." Deacon handed her a faded book covered with pink fabric. On the pages within, Emily detailed her relationship with first Raney, then Davidson, and what she'd uncovered during those times. *They told me if I spoke out, they would ruin me. I don't feel safe. I can't trust anyone,*" Bella read.

Deacon placed a steady hand on her shoulder as Bella's phone rang. She reached up and patted his hand, then retrieved her phone from the pocket of her jeans.

"Are the two of you about done?" Shea asked, her voice steady but tinged with worry.

"Yes." Bella explained what they'd found.

"Davidson's father took control of Emily's family's land shortly after her death," Deacon said. "Here's a transcript of a phone call. Bella, it appears your grandmother had hired a private investigator to dig up these facts a long time ago."

She glanced at the transcript. "*She's a liability. We can't afford her running her mouth,*'" Raney said. '*We'll handle it. Accidents happen all the time. Everyone knows how much she loves the lake behind the inn.*'"

Bella grabbed a box from on top of the armoire and set the evidence inside. In her opinion, they now had an ironclad case against the older Davidson and Raney.

Another call from Shea alerted them to the fact they had company.

"We can't risk this falling into the wrong hands." Bella shoved the box into the armoire. "We'll let the sheriff come retrieve it."

"Good idea." Deacon took her hand and led her out of the passageway and back to the kitchen.

The company turned out to be Wells returning from wherever it was the man went. By the time he entered the kitchen, Bella and Deacon were sipping cups of coffee while sitting at the kitchen island.

Bella focused on regulating her heartbeat, afraid the man could hear it beating. "There's coffee if you want it."

"I noticed you have another guest."

Bella nodded. "Just for a bit until she finds

property to purchase."

Shea moved up behind him. "You wouldn't know of any, would you?" Her smile didn't quite reach her eyes.

"No, but I'm not intending to put down roots in Misty Hollow." Declining the offer of coffee, he left the kitchen.

"I'm going to have someone dig into his background," Shea said softly. "There's something off about that man. Ready to head to the sheriff's office?"

"Yep." Bella slid from the stool, leaving her cup on the counter. "We decided to leave the evidence where we found it."

The scuff of a shoe sounded outside the kitchen.

Shea pulled a gun from the waistband of her slacks and peered out the door. She pulled back and frowned. "I think your guest was eavesdropping. The sooner we alert Westbrook, the better."

They rushed to Deacon's truck, which sported a brand-new back window, and climbed in. Shea sat in the back seat. Her constant glancing out the window kept Bella's nerves on edge.

When they arrived at the sheriff's department, the receptionist shook her head. "You might as well rent space you're here so much. Go on back. The sheriff is free."

Westbrook listened quietly while they told him what they'd found and where it was hidden. "I'll send someone over to get it," he said when they'd finished. "You should also know Garrett Boyd has skipped town. Moved out of the hotel in the middle of the night. I'll bring Raney in for questioning and head to the nursing home myself. Watch your backs. You've stirred up a hornet's nest."

~

"Wanna grab some lunch?" Deacon glanced at Bella, then in the rearview mirror at Shea.

"You are always hungry." Bella laughed.

"So?" He grinned.

"Yes, let's go to the diner. Shea can talk to Lucy about property for sale."

Shea insisted on sitting where she could see the door, leaving the other side of the booth for Deacon and Bella to squeeze into. Deacon wasn't complaining. He liked the way her leg pressed against his.

When their server came, they placed their orders and asked to speak to Lucy. The owner of the diner, her hair freshly dyed a vibrant red, approached the table. "You wanted to speak to me?"

Shea introduced herself, asking that Lucy keep her identity to herself for now. "I'm looking for a house on a bit of property where I can keep a horse. These two said you might be able to help me."

"Absolutely. Be right back." She returned a few minutes later with an old man in faded jeans and a flannel shirt. "Alfred, this lady might be interested in buying your place."

"Really?" He grinned, revealing gaps from missing teeth. "Great. I want to move to Florida to be near by daughter. Here's the address and asking price." He pulled a folded flier from his pocket. "I was just about to post this on Lucy's board over there. It has two bedrooms and two full bathrooms."

Shea smiled. "We'll head over there to take a look once we've finished eating. Thank you."

He nodded and left the diner.

"Could it really be that easy?" She asked.

"Some things are." Deacon nodded. "I sure hope you'll stay at the inn until the danger is past."

"I will."

Once they finished eating, Deacon drove them to the address on the flier. Five acres, part of it wooded, backed up to government land. An A-frame-style house sat at the end of a dirt road. A small red barn sat off to one side.

"This looks perfect." Shea climbed from the truck and marched up to the house as Alfred came out.

"Come on in." He grinned and waved them inside. "It's a little messy. Stays that way now that the missus is gone, but you get the picture. All the furniture stays. I'm only taking my keepsakes."

"I'll take it." Shea thrust out her hand.

"No haggling over the price?" His bushy brows rose.

"No, sir, it's a fair price."

"Then, it's yours. I'll be gone in a couple of weeks. We can transfer the deed at the bank next week. Welcome home." He returned her handshake.

Deacon couldn't help but feel a twinge of envy. The house was sufficient for his needs, but he did want more than five acres. What he wanted would come along when the time was right.

He glanced at Bella. Staying with her at the inn for the rest of his life seemed a very good alternative. Hopefully, he'd have the chance to take her on that first date they'd spoken about.

Halfway to the inn, a truck with oversized tires loomed behind them, filling the view in Deacon's rearview mirror. He narrowed his eyes and accelerated.

Shea turned to look out the back. "Do you know that vehicle?"

"Nope." He couldn't go faster on the hairpin curves.

The truck rammed them, snapping his head forward. A man in a ski mask hung out the passenger side window and aimed a rifle.

"Get down." Shea squeezed into the front seat between Bella and the door before aiming her handgun out the window. "Whatever you do, Deacon, do not stop."

"I don't plan on it." His knuckles whitened at his tight grip on the steering wheel.

The rifle fired.

Shea returned fire.

Deacon's new window shattered, once again peppering him with glass. His insurance company was going to have a field day.

The truck behind them swerved as Shea shot out one of its tires before careening into the ditch and into a tree. Shea returned to the back seat, swiping glass to the floor.

Now that the truth no longer hid in the shadows, he and Bella had to fight to survive.

Chapter Fifteen

Bella and the others sat in Deacon's truck and watched as two sheriff department cars and an ambulance arrived at the crash scene. Both men, one of them Thomas Wells, climbed into the ambulance unassisted. She doubted the same would have been possible the other way around. Bella, Deacon, and Shea would've been executed in the crumpled vehicle.

"Guess I won't be paid by my first guest."

Deacon gave her a wide-eyed look, then laughed. "Be glad you're alive to take in more guests."

"Oh, I am." She returned his smile which faded when Sheriff Westbrook approached them.

"Everyone all right?" He peered into the cab of the truck.

"All good here," Shea said. "Are we free to go?"

"Yes, but come into the station tomorrow so we can take your statements." He grinned at Shea. "You sure you want to take on this town?"

She returned his grin with a rare one of her own. "I might be having second thoughts."

"Don't you dare. I'm ready to spend more time with my wife, my kids, and my fishing pole."

Laughing, he slapped the hood of the truck and sauntered back to his car.

"I'll wait until morning to clean out Wells's room." Bella leaned her head against the seat. "How many more men are on Raney's payroll?"

Deacon took her hand in his, gave a gentle squeeze, then drove away from the crash. "Hopefully, not too many more. I'm ready for justice to be served for Emily and Mildred."

No more than she was.

"I have coffee and pound cake," Ida told them the moment they walked in the door. "Sit and relax before heading to bed."

"You're a godsend." Bella gave her a quick hug. "Hiring you was one of the best things I've ever done."

"Oh, go on now." The woman beamed. "Keith took care of the horses, then headed out for the night. I told him it was okay." She winked. "I think he has a girlfriend."

"As long as he isn't on Raney's payroll, too." Bella bit into a slice of lemon pound cake with lemon drizzled icing.

"I know his mother. He's a good boy." Ida removed her apron and draped it over a chair. "Rufus said he was going to bed early, which sounds like a good idea to me. See you in the morning."

Once the cook left, Deacon turned to Bella. "She's right. I checked the young man out thoroughly before sending him to you."

Bella sighed. "I know you did. It's just that I'm finding it hard to trust anyone right now. Other than you and Shea." She turned to glance at the new sheriff. "I read about your ordeal on the other side of Misty

Mountain. Pardon my language, but you are one kickass woman."

Shea shrugged. "I did what had to be done and don't think about it anymore than I have to."

"I'm glad to have you on our side."

"Thank you." Shea took her coffee and slice of cake to the back deck.

"She prefers to be alone," Bella said.

"Regardless of her saying she doesn't like to think about that time, I bet she thinks about it a lot." Deacon sat next to Bella. "You don't kill someone easily and not dwell on it unless you're a monster."

Bella's head tilted "Wonder if I could kill someone if I had to? Maybe. I hope I'm as strong as Shea is if the situation warrants."

"You're a very strong woman." His brow furrowed. "Look at how much you've accomplished in the short time you've been here."

"I couldn't have done it without you." She didn't know what she would do when he left. He helped far more than just around the inn. His support during this dangerous time meant a lot. "I'm heading to bed." Bella slid from the stool. "Good night. Come, Ghost."

"I'll lock up down here," Deacon said.

Shea returned to the kitchen with her dog, Heidi. "Bed sounds very good to me." She wished them good luck and followed Bella upstairs.

"Sorry you're stuck here instead of settling into your new place." Bella paused, her hand on the door of her room.

"It's fine. The papers haven't been signed yet anyway. We'll put an end to all this soon enough." With a nod, Shea entered her room across the hall and closed the door.

With a heavy sigh, Bella went into her own room, locking the door behind her. Not because she feared those staying under the same roof, but because of those who didn't.

The trouble surrounding her affected others. Raney needed to be stopped, but she had no idea how. They'd turned over plenty of evidence to the authorities. What was the sheriff waiting for?

Bella changed into cotton pajamas and climbed under the blankets. Apparently, the sheriff needed to find the right time to arrest Raney, but for how long? Impatience plagued her as she stared at the ceiling for a few minutes before turning off her bedside lamp.

Dare she ask Sheriff Westbrook what the delay was? Would he even tell her?

~

Deacon waited up a while after the women went to bed. He walked the perimeter of the property, making sure things were as they should be. Still, he couldn't help the nagging feeling that something wasn't right. He should've brought Ghost or Heidi with him.

Not finding anything amiss, he returned to the house and made sure the doors and windows were locked. As he double-checked the front door, a flicker of movement outside drew his attention.

He dimmed the lights he had yet to turn off and waited for his eyes to adjust to the darkness. The crunch of footsteps on gravel reached his ears.

Shea moved like a wraith down the stairs. "Someone outside?"

"How did you know?"

"Saw them flitting around through the trees. I

counted three."

"Wake up the others, please. I'll contact Rufus to stay where he is." Deacon pulled out his phone as Shea rushed back up the stairs.

By the time he'd texted both Rufus and the sheriff, a sleepy Bella joined him downstairs. "What is it?"

"Trouble." He peered back outside.

Raney stood in the light of the moon and stared at the inn. Two men, both carrying gas cans, fanned out on either side of him.

"They're going to set the inn on fire."

"No!" Bella gasped as she raced for the back door. "It's blocked."

Deacon moved to a window that allowed him a partial view of the front door. A large beam had been propped against it. They must've blocked the front while he was scouting around outside, then done the same with the back door after he entered the house.

"Let's hope help comes quickly." The area hadn't had rain in a couple of weeks, and a fire would spread fast. "Can we climb out of one of the bedroom windows?"

"Not with the dogs." Bella frowned. "I won't leave Ghost."

Of course, she wouldn't. He doubted Shea would leave her dog behind either. By the time they fashioned a harness to lower the animals, they'd be sitting ducks. "Wet towels and blankets and put around the bases of the doors. Soak the doors the best you can. I'm going to yank down curtains." It would leave them exposed to gunfire, but he'd prefer a bullet over being burned to death.

As he pulled a set of curtains down, he came face-to-face with a masked man dousing the outer wall with gasoline. When Deacon reached for the gun at his waist, the man threw down a match and raced out of sight.

"We might be safe in the lowest passage under this house," Shea said. "It has dirt walls."

"Let's go. Bella, come on." They rushed to a closet under the stairs and descended into darkness. He used his phone as a flashlight and prayed they'd managed to wet things enough, so the inn wasn't a total loss.

"I can't believe I'm going to lose everything." Bella started to turn back. "I need to do more."

Deacon reached out and stopped her. "You'll die up there."

"I have to try." She yanked free and raced back up the wooden steps, Deacon on her heels.

Already smoke seeped under the front and back doors. A window shattered. Bella screamed and jumped back before running to the kitchen. "Ida!"

The cook was filling buckets and bowls with water.

"Why didn't you come down with us?" Deacon narrowed his eyes.

"And let this place burn? Get busy. I might be foolish, but this inn has been here a long time, and no fool is going to burn it to the ground."

The group frantically splashed water at each window and door. Deacon's arms were aching when he finally heard the welcome sound of a siren. Knowing the men who'd started the fire would be long gone, he put a wet towel over his head and opened the front door. After leaping over the flames, Deacon grabbed the water hose from the side of the house and sprayed the flames licking at the porch.

Within minutes, Shea aimed a hose on the back while Bella and Ida huddled together a few yards away.

A fire truck pulled up on the driveway, and firemen jumped from the vehicle. Soon, strong plumes of water inundated the inn's exterior. Deacon dropped the hose and joined the women. "The fire didn't get inside. You'll have some smoke damage and need repairs to the siding, but the inn will live to see another day."

Bella leaned into him, and he put his arm around her. With a sob, she buried her face in his chest. "I can't lose this inn. I just can't."

"I know, darlin'." He rested his chin on her head, turning when the sheriff arrived.

"How many?" He pulled a notepad from inside his pocket.

"Three. One of them Raney."

The sheriff's eyes widened. "Are you sure?"

"Positive. He didn't seem to care that we saw him. Raney was the only one not wearing a mask. They'd blocked the doors. I was only able to get out the front because the beam braced against the door had burned enough. They intended us to burn alive."

Bella faced the sheriff. "Why haven't you arrested Raney yet? We gave you all the evidence you need."

"I sure hope you made copies because that evidence disappeared." A muscle ticked his jaw.

"What?" Deacon stiffened. "Wasn't it locked up?"

"Yep. Which means I've got a dirty mole in my department."

"Anyone new?" Shea asked.

"A couple. I've been watching them closely since

this all began. Both have alibis for tonight, and I don't have a definite time when the evidence disappeared." He shoved the notepad back into his pocket. "I will find out who he is, though. It's got to be one of two. Plus, I've hired a new deputy sheriff who will start tomorrow. He's coming from Houston, so it can't be him."

"How do you know?" Deacon tilted his head.

"Because he's the son of a very close friend. I've known him since he was a boy. My bet is on Bolton. All I have to do is prove it. I suggest the three of you find somewhere else to stay until you take care of the smoke and water damage." He spun around and marched to his car.

"Now what?" Bella faced Deacon.

"We make copies of the evidence on your phone and hand it to the sheriff."

"My phone is on my nightstand. I'll go pack a bag." Her shoulders slumped as she entered the house.

"I need to start spending time at the office." Shea's jaw tightened. "Find out more about those two deputies the sheriff suspects. No more hiding my identity."

"Sounds good." Deacon headed inside to gather his things. Should they head to a motel or take their troubles to the ranch?

Chapter Sixteen

The motel manager hadn't been very accommodating about letting two large dogs stay in one of his rooms, but Shea's badge convinced him otherwise. Now, Bella stood in the doorway of a room that hadn't been updated since the 1970s.

Worn golden shag carpet, a psychedelic gold and green bedspread that clashed with the striped wallpaper of the same color. Through the open bathroom door, she spotted gold bathroom fixtures. At least it was clean.

She tossed her overnight bag and laptop on the bed she'd share with Shea, leaving the other bed for Deacon. Ghost would have to be content to sleep on the floor instead of curled next to her.

Tomorrow's top priority would be to find where Raney hid. It couldn't be far. Not if he hoped to stop word of his corruption getting out. His and his father's.

"This is interesting." Deacon motioned for her to look out the window.

Deputy Bolton stood talking to the manager outside the motel office. The deputy handed manager something before the manager pointed to the room where Bella and the others stayed. "Here comes our dirty cop."

"Yep." Deacon snapped a photo with his phone. "I'll send this to the sheriff. Why don't the two of you get some sleep. We'll take turns keeping watch."

"Why not leave?"

"And go where? Bolton knows we're here. He won't let us leave alive." He tapped on his phone. "It's best we wait until the sheriff arrives."

"I agree." Shea plopped down into one of the two chairs in the room and checked the ammo in her gun. "We'll be shot if we go out. In a few minutes, I suspect there will be more than Bolton waiting for us."

The air conditioner clicked on and rattled so loudly Bella doubted she'd be able to fall asleep. Still, she curled up on the bed and closed her eyes hoping to get a few hours of sleep. Throughout the night, she'd wake to see either Deacon or Shea keeping watch. Why hadn't the sheriff come to their aid? Was he dirty as well?

The sound of glass shattering outside, then the blaring of a car alarm catapulted her from bed.

Heavy footsteps pounded outside the door. Deacon jumped back as a rock flew through the window littering the shag carpet with glass.

"What's going on?" Bella hugged a pillow to her chest.

Both dogs barked, teeth bared at the door.

"Hush," Shea ordered. "Five men outside are playing games. Bolton left an hour ago."

"Where's Sheriff Westbrook?"

"Dealing with a rash of petty crime in town." Her features set in grave lines. "Help won't be coming for a while."

"I might be able to squeeze through the bathroom window and drive for help." She had to do something.

"All four tires on my truck have been slashed." Deacon peered back out the window. "You wouldn't stand a chance on foot."

Bella posted her fists on her hips. "I would if they didn't see me."

"No." Shea's voice left little room for argument. "During my trouble up on that mountain, one of my friends took off alone and almost died. She should've died. Would have if I hadn't gone after her. We stick together."

Bella huffed, knowing the new sheriff was right, but she felt useless. She pushed away from the bed and went to make coffee. That she could do. "Did Sheriff Westbrook say what kind of trouble there was in town?"

"Someone broke into the sheriff's station, tied up the night receptionist, and locked the one deputy there in a holding cell." Deacon continued to stare out the window. "Store windows are being broken, cars stolen…a bunch of things intended to keep the sheriff and the deputies anywhere but here."

"What did they take from the sheriff's department?" She handed him a paper cup of coffee, then went to fill one for Shea.

"The sheriff texted that they nabbed the copies he'd made of the files that had been stolen." Shea gave a wry smile. "So, Deacon sent them again. The fools outside must know there are other copies there. Killing us won't stop the files from getting out."

A barrage of gunfire erupted.

Deacon tackled Bella to the floor, knocking over a

lamp and breaking the bulb. The room darkened.

Bella had never been more terrified or felt more safe than she did at that moment. Deacon lying across her, wrapping her in his arms, felt like a warm blanket. It didn't take long for his weight to grow heavy, and she squirmed. "I can't breathe."

"Sorry." He eased the pressure. "Scoot between the two beds. They'll provide some protection."

"Here, Ghost." She crawled between the two beds. "Heidi." With both dogs beside her, she sat and waited for whatever would come next.

When the shooting stopped, Deacon and Shea once again stood guard at the window. Bella remained where she was, again feeling useless.

Her mind drifted to the work that would be needed to repair the inn after the fire. The renovations she'd already made had eaten away at the funds her grandmother left her. The repairs that needed doing now would use up the rest. She ticked off the needed repairs, trying to take her mind off what was happening outside. It didn't work. Every noise on the other side of the door made her stiffen. Would this trouble ever end?

"Let me see your phone, Deacon."

"For?" His brow arched.

"I want to dig through everything in those files we sent and try to find out where Raney might be hiding."

~

Deacon should've taken the women to the ranch. He'd have backup there. He contemplated sending a text to his boss and promptly rejected the idea. The danger was too great to involve someone else.

"Raney has a lakeside cabin under his maternal grandfather's name," Bella said. "I bet he's hiding there. I'll let the sheriff know."

"Good job." He shot her a smile before turning his gaze back to the window.

Five men now leaned against a vehicle smoking as if they hadn't just shot up the motel. The manager sent the men a single wave, climbed into a battered sedan, and sped away. Lucky man.

Deacon glanced at the clock on the wall. Two a.m. It might be daybreak before help arrived, which meant at least four more hours stuck in a room where they had no other choice but to wait. The men outside seemed to be holding off until they received further orders. Until then, Deacon and the rest in the motel room would have some peace.

He contemplated Bella's idea about her fleeing through the bathroom window. Shea's story concerned him, but Bella would have a better chance at survival away from the motel. If anyone should survive, it was the woman he was quickly falling in love with. "Bella should run."

Both women looked his way with wide eyes. "Didn't you hear what I told you?" Shea asked.

"I did, but it's quite possible we'll all die here before help arrives. She's the only one who will fit through that window. You and I can create a distraction until she reaches the woods." As badly as he wanted her away from the motel, the thought of her alone in unfamiliar woods sent ice through his veins.

"The sheriff's department is occupied." Shea shook her head. "It's a suicide mission."

"Bella isn't going to the sheriff. She's going to my friend, Dave Wakes, who leads a motorcycle gang. They've come to the aid of more than one resident of

Misty Hollow. The five men outside won't be any match for Dave and his riders."

"Then text him."

"I have, but he hasn't responded. I still want Bella to get out of here for her own safety."

Bella bounded to her feet and rushed to the bathroom. "The coast is clear. I can easily make it to the cover of the trees."

Deacon and Shea followed her. "Make haste. I've texted you Dave's address. You can find him easily enough." He cupped her face. "Be safe."

"Don't worry." She caressed his cheek. "I'll be fine. Just in case, let's use a tracking app so you'll know where I am."

Why hadn't he thought of that? "You're a smart woman, Isabella Harper."

She grinned and installed the app. "See? You'll know where I am within twenty yards."

The app eased some of his apprehension. He slid the window open. "Ghost first." The dog struggled, clearly not wanting to leave Bella behind.

"Good boy." Bella climbed onto the toilet tank, then glanced at Deacon and Shea. "I'll be fine." Her voice shook. "I'm not alone as long as I have Ghost."

Shea nodded. "He's more than my friend had."

With a grim smile, Bella squeezed through the window.

Time for that distraction. Deacon moved back to the front window and started firing, shooting out the two front tires of the men's vehicle, then he ducked when they returned fire. When he straightened, the five men had taken cover behind the car.

"You really think she'll find your friend before the

sheriff arrives?" Shea gave him a dubious look.

He shrugged. "Maybe not, but at least she isn't here. Sorry you're involved."

"This isn't your fight either, yet here you are."

"I love her."

"You might never have the chance to tell her. I'm here because it's my job. Your emotions will be your pitfall."

The ache in his gut intensified. "I know." He quirked a smile. "I have a feeling you'd be here even if it wasn't your job."

Her eyes widened. "What makes you think so?"

"It's the type of person you are."

She chuckled. "Maybe you're right. I did go into law enforcement to serve and protect. I haven't done a very good job of protecting the two of you, have I?"

"We're still breathing, aren't we?" He gave a short laugh. "We only have to hang on for a few more hours."

"How much ammo do you have? I'm down to two bullets."

He checked his gun. "Three."

The odds weren't looking good.

Chapter Seventeen

Bella landed with a soft thud outside the motel bathroom window. Ghost whined and pressed against her.

"Come on, boy. We have work to do." Without looking back, she sprinted for the stand of trees a few yards away. When no cry of alarm came, she slowed her pace just enough to lessen the risk of falling or twisting an ankle. She couldn't slow down too much. Deacon and Shea's survival might depend on her finding the biker. If something happened to Deacon because Bella failed, she'd never be able to live with herself because...she loved him.

The sudden knowledge shocked her. The love she felt for him had come slowly, building during the time they spent together, then strengthening under his protection. Now, it was her turn to protect him.

Visibility could be better, but she couldn't wait for sunrise. The woods seemed alive with the pulse of her fear. Danger lurked in the darkness. She could've used a flashlight, but that would only show any possible pursuers her location.

A twig snapped behind her, sending her heart into her throat. Ghost's ears twitched, but he didn't show any signs of someone pursuing them.

"Find the way, Ghost." Bella was more than willing to let her trusty canine find the way to the road. Every so often, she glanced at the GPS on her phone to make sure they were going in the right direction. Occasionally, she had to redirect Ghost.

They stepped into a clearing as the sun peeked over the horizon. Shouts cut through the silence. Flashlights blinded her. Ghost barked and took a protective stance in front of her. Bella's heart sank. They were surrounded.

One of the men aimed his gun at Ghost.

"No, please." Bella raised her hands. "I'll send him away. Don't shoot my dog."

The man jerked his gun toward the trees.

"Go, Ghost. Now!"

The dog whined and implored her with his dark eyes. When she ordered him again, he slunk away. Tears blurred Bella's vision as another man bound her hands behind her with zip ties.

"Raney wants to talk to you," the man said, jerking her after him.

They shoved her into a van. Why was it always a van?

She felt around the darkness for something to cut through the ties. The back of the vehicle was empty.

After what seemed like an eternity, the van stopped. The back door opened, letting in the harsh rays of the sun which blinded her momentarily. Then one of the men dragged her out. He dropped her to her knees in front of a cabin.

She glanced around for anything, any place that could help her. Out of the corner of her eye, she spotted the shimmer of a river or lake from behind the trees. If she could manage to get free, she knew how to get home. The problem would be getting free.

The door of the cabin opened, and Raney stepped onto the sweeping porch. She almost didn't recognize him in jeans and a flannel shirt. Face grim, he strode toward her. "Give me your phone."

"That's hard to do with my hands tied." She grinned, despite the fear threatening to choke her.

He felt in the pockets of her jeans until he found it.

"That's a bit personal. I don't even know you."

He glared, then smashed the phone under his boot. "Take her in the house."

Someone behind her hauled her to her feet and pushed her onto the porch and into the cabin This was no mayor's cabin. Sparsely furnished and decorated, it appeared to be someone's vacation home. Deacon would have no way of knowing which lake cabin Raney held her in.

How long until someone missed her? Could Ghost find his way back to the motel and get help? He might be able to lead Deacon and the sheriff to the clearing where she'd been taken but no further.

Would the tracking app show her last location? That was her only hope.

Raney motioned for her to sit in a straight-backed chair, then sat in front of her, his gaze sharp. "Who all has the evidence you found?"

"Me, Deacon, and the sheriff." She tilted her head. "You plan on killing all three of us?"

"If I have to. I cannot have this town find out what my father did all those years ago."

"Why not just let him take the fall? Now that

you've kidnapped me, sent men to burn the inn…and killed my grandmother—" She swallowed past the lump in her throat. "You're now as guilty as he is."

"I did what needed doing to keep my family name clean."

"Doesn't look like you did a very good job." She didn't see the slap coming. Her head snapped to the side.

"You've put me in a bind, Miss Harper."

"It's not personal." Liar—it was so personal. "I only want justice for my grandmother and Emily Marks."

"Why does something that happened so long ago matter?" His brow furrowed. "You didn't know Emily."

"Because what happened to both my grandmother and Emily was wrong—first degree murder wrong."

"And look where justice has gotten you."

"How did you know where to find me?"

He laughed. "I'm smarter than you think. I had someone watching the back of the motel in case one of you tried to escape."

~

Finally. The sheriff and his deputies arrived, arresting the five men who had held Deacon and Shea hostage in the motel.

Deacon stepped outside to greet Westbrook. "Have you seen or heard from Bella?" It had been almost two hours.

"No. I thought she was here with you."

"We sent her out the back window."

A bark drew his attention as Ghost darted from around the motel. Deacon's heart dropped. The dog would not leave Bella unless something had happened.

He pulled out his phone and opened the tracking app. "Her last known location was by the lake."

"We can't go in cars," the sheriff said. "They'll kill her as soon as we show up."

"I can call for some horses from the Rocking W."

Sheriff Westbrook turned to Shea. "You want to go with Deacon or stay and book those men?"

"Since you assigned me protection detail, I'd like to finish the job."

Deacon called the Rocking W and requested three horses. They'd arrive in less than thirty minutes with a couple of the ranch hands to help with the search. How could he stay still for that long when Bella was in danger?

The sheriff stepped away to let his deputies know the plan. Soon, cars with the five men pulled away from the motel. "I also told them to find the motel manager. He'll be arrested for aiding and abetting by taking a bribe. Bolton never returned to the office. I've put out a BOLO on both of them."

Shea went to the vending machine near the office and returned with sodas and chips. "Since I'm hungry, I figured you probably were too."

"Thanks." Deacon popped the tab and guzzled the soda.

Shea watered both dogs, then sat on the hood of his truck to eat her chips. She stared into the distance, a haunted look on her face.

"She's struggling with what happened on the mountain," Deacon said.

"Good. Since she doesn't like killing, she'll be a good sheriff. You don't want one who kills easily." He removed his hat, ran his hand through his hair, then replaced the hat.

"You're a good sheriff."

He grinned. "I'll still be around if I'm needed."

Knowing Westbrook didn't intend to go far gave Deacon a measure of comfort. While they waited on the horses, he thought about the future. He couldn't contemplate one without Bella. Not after getting to know her.

What about his dream of owning his own land? Could he be content helping Bella run the inn? Deacon prayed Bella would be there to share his life—whatever direction it took. He pushed away from his truck with the flattened tires and shattered window as two horse trailers pulled up. Maverick and River jumped out and unloaded five horses.

Once they were all in the saddle, Deacon told Ghost to find Bella. The dog shot toward the woods not stopping until they reached a clearing. Then, nose to the ground, he searched until he picked up her scent again. The trail was lost at the highway.

No matter. They didn't need the highway to find her, but now they knew where she'd been taken from. He gave the others the coordinates of Bella's last location and ordered Ghost to follow. It would take them an hour on horseback.

Hang on, Bella. I'm coming.

Their horses plodded through the woods when the brush was thick and trotted when the terrain allowed. No one spoke, the only sounds coming from the creak of their saddles and the plod of hooves. They crossed the highway at one point, earning the blaring of horns as cars passed, then crossed a couple of dirt roads. The sun rose higher in the sky warming the early autumn day.

Deacon wanted to gallop. The only thing holding him back was the threat of injury to his horse. The more time passed, the more he feared that they would be too late. He should never have let her go out the window. She wasn't familiar with the territory and hadn't gotten far before being abducted. This was all his fault.

Ghost flitted in and out of the trees like a wraith. He'd trot ahead, then return, shooting Deacon looks that implored him to move faster. Deacon longed to reassure the dog that Bella would be okay, but how could he when he wondered himself?

"Stop blaming yourself," Shea said softly. "She volunteered."

"I could've stopped her."

"How?" She arched a brow. "Bella strikes me as a woman who does what she wants. I didn't want her to go either. What I feared would happen did. But, I couldn't stop her any more than you could. Her bravery is one of the things you love about her."

True. He nodded. "I hope I get the chance to tell her so."

Shea fell back, leaving him once again to his thoughts. The woman was right. Bella would do what she wanted.

He'd hold onto the hope that Bella would find a way to survive until he got there.

Chapter Eighteen

Raney's frantic pacing and constant glances out the window set Bella's nerves on edge. He was waiting for something, and she didn't think it would bode well for her.

"What are you looking for?" Her blood chilled as he whipped around to face her.

"My ride out of here. I've got a plane waiting at an abandoned airstrip a few miles away." He gave her a shark-like grin. "Then, it's curtains for you."

"Why not kill me now?"

"I might need you for a while longer."

A horse nickered outside. Did the man plan on leaving by car or animal? Hurry, Deacon. Even with her phone being smashed, the app should still show her last location. She didn't know how much longer she had.

Killing her wouldn't free Raney of criminal prosecution. Now, it was all about revenge.

She hung her head. *I'm sorry, Grandma. I did my best.*

"Head up." Raney sneered. He had the smile of a predator which told her he relished her fear.

She forced herself to breathe steadily. There had to

be a way out. All she had to do was keep a level head and think. Her gaze landed on a broken beer bottle sticking out from under the sofa. It might work if she could get to it.

Headlights flashed through the window, sweeping across the room. Raney stopped his pacing. His posture stiffened.

Bella's breath caught. Was it help or the ride Raney waited for?

As soon as Raney stepped outside, she rushed to the beer bottle. Her hands sweated as she tried to pick it up. Not an easy task with her hands secured behind her back.

The sharp edge cut into her wrists as she used the bottle to cut through the zip tie. She ignored the pain as voices drifted through the open door of the cabin. Loud voices. Raney argued with someone. The other man's voice sounded familiar, but she couldn't place him.

Before she could free herself, the door flew open with a bang against the door.

"What are you doing?" Raney yanked her to her feet and knocked the bottle from her hands. "We've got to go now."

The vehicle outside drove away.

Gunshots rang out.

Raney dragged Bella to the back door. "We're leaving on horseback."

"I can't ride with my hands behind my back."

"You'd better figure it out." He pulled her against his chest, using her as a shield.

~

Ghost stopped, his ears standing at attention. Deacon raised his fist for those with him to stop. He slid from the saddle and parted the thick brush.

A cluster of men stood near the front porch of a modest cabin. Several horses milled about in a small corral near the back of the building. A van, most likely the one used to transport Bella, sat parked out front. "Stay, Ghost," he whispered before returning to the others.

"I count five men. No sign of Raney, but he's probably inside with Bella. What's our next move?" He glanced up at Sheriff Westbrook.

"We need to move carefully in order to save Bella. Raney is a caged animal right now. Once he realizes we're here he may kill her."

If he hadn't already. No. Deacon wouldn't think that way. He swung back into the saddle and waited for the sheriff's instructions.

Headlights broke through the trees. "Raney is now on the porch," Sheriff Westbrook said. "Wait for my signal. It's Bolton. Shoot the tires on that truck."

Deacon aimed through the trees and fired. Raney's men scattered and made a run for the horses. Bolton fell from his vehicle and sprinted after the other men.

From the back of the house, Deacon spotted Raney and Bella on horseback fleeing away from the cabin. Without a second thought, he dug his heels into his horse and took off after them.

The thunder of his horse's hooves and the barking of Ghost running at his side drowned out all other sound. The only thought running through Deacon's mind was to reach Bella before he lost her forever.

His mouth fell open as she slid from the back of the racing horse. Just as Deacon started to rein his horse to a stop, Shea slid from her saddle. "I'll look after

Bella. Go get Raney."

His gaze landed on Bella who offered a weak smile. "I'm fine. Just got the wind knocked out of me. Get him."

Deacon nodded, leaving Bella in the care of Shea and Ghost. He wasn't law enforcement. It should be Shea giving chase. What kept him going was the anger surging through him at what Raney put Bella through.

Raney turned in the saddle and fired, striking a nearby tree. Bark struck Deacon in the face. He returned fire. The force of the shot must have knocked Raney from his horse.

Deacon leaped from the saddle, kicked the gun out of Raney's hand, and aimed his weapon at the man's head. "On your feet. You can't get away. The sheriff and his men are rounding up your men, including Bolton. It's over."

"It'll never be over," he growled.

"Sure it will. You will spend the rest of your life in jail. So will the senior Davidson. On. Your. Feet."

Raney struggled to stand, finally getting up. He pressed a hand to the hole in his shoulder. "I need medical attention."

"You'll get what you need." Deacon climbed back in the saddle, keeping his gun on Raney. "Start walking."

It seemed like an eternity before the cabin came into view. Sheriff Westbrook promptly took possession of Raney, leaving Deacon free to check on Bella.

She sat on the steps of the cabin porch while an EMT checked her over. "You got him." Her smile was glorious.

"Sure did." Deacon sat next to her. "How are

you?"

"Might have a cracked rib or two, but other than that, I'm fine. Landed on my elbow when I fell off the horse." She shrugged. "I had to. I couldn't let him get away with me."

He caressed the bruise on her cheek, then ran his thumb over the split on her lip. "He hit you."

She grinned. "I smarted off."

"That's my girl. I'm so sorry." Deacon cupped her face in his hands and kissed her lightly, mindful of her injuries. He'd have the rest of his life to kiss her soundly.

Epilogue

A few nights later, Deacon and Isabella stepped outside the inn. The night had fully settled over the lake, a dark but serene mirror reflecting a sky full of stars—quiet witnesses to the peace that had been restored.

Bella leaned into Deacon as his arm wrapped around her waist. "I have a full ledger of reservations, both for the inn and the venue." She gazed up at him. "Thank you. I couldn't have done it without you. None of it."

"You'd have figured out a way." He smiled down at her.

She shook her head. "I might've given up. Sold the inn after the danger escalated."

"You don't give yourself enough credit, sweetheart." Keeping his arms around her, he turned her around to face him. "I know I've never taken you on that date I promised. Not yet, anyway, but...do you think you could stand having me around?"

Her heart skipped a beat. "What do you mean?"

"Once, I'd had a dream of owning my own land, raising horses, maybe a few cattle. That dream has changed."

"What's your dream now?" Her voice faltered, not sure she wanted to hear what he said.

"I want to help you run the inn. Increase the services we can offer. I love you, Isabella Harper, and I want to spend the rest of my life with you. Will you let me?"

She smiled and tapped her finger against her cheek. "Hmmm. Let me think for a minute."

His brow furrowed. Apprehension flickered in his eyes.

She laughed. "Are you asking me to marry you?"

"Yes, but only if you intend to say yes."

"Of course, I'll say yes. Didn't I just tell you I couldn't manage without you? The thought of not having you here with me every day fills me with sadness." Tears blurred her vision. "I love you and have for a while now. Maybe our wedding should be the first one in the venue. We'll have to act fast, though. As I said, we have a waiting list."

"You tell me when, and I'll be there." He lowered his head and kissed her soundly.

The End

If you'd like to know more about the new sheriff, Shea Callahan, you can in *Girls' Weekend Survival* <u>here</u>.

Chapter One

Shea Callahan tossed a battered duffel bag and backpack into the back of the rental van her soccer-mom friend, Becky, had rented. She winced. A girls' weekend in the mountains should be a welcome retreat, but her mind wouldn't stop straying to how the folks of Misty Hollow would react to their new sheriff being a woman. She unzipped the bag, checked her handgun, then zipped the bag back up and closed the back of the van. Would the residents of Misty Hollow think she could handle the rash of crime that had plagued the town in the last few years?

"That's the last of it." Becky grinned and opened the driver's side door. "You sure you don't want to drive?"

"I'll take the next shift." She glanced at the mound of luggage. Way too much for a simple weekend away.

"Got your inhaler?"

Shea frowned. "Yes, Mom."

"Sorry. It's a habit." Becky grinned.

"I'm so glad we managed to do this." Emma, the cheerleader of the group, slid into the backseat. "The ten of us have talked about this since college. It's about time, don't you think?"

Tessa, expansive braids swinging, climbed in next. "I have to admit to being a bit nervous to stay on Misty Mountain. Too many things have happened up there." She glanced back at Shea. "You sure you want to work in that town?"

"I'm sure." After the way good ole Southern boys treated a woman deputy, a small, secluded town sounded perfect. Hopefully Shea could prove her worth without prejudice. She tied her long, dark hair into a messy bun, then climbed into the front passenger seat since she always got car sick in the back. She felt her pocket to make sure she hadn't forgotten her inhaler, then clicked her seatbelt into place.

"Yay!" Becky started the engine. "This weekend is going to be great."

Despite wishing she could spend the next few days preparing for her new job, Shea smiled. She loved these women and would do her best to focus on having a good time with them.

"Shea, Tessa, Becky, Lauren, Melanie, Annie, Deborah, Kara, Rachel, and me," Emma counted. "The terrific ten set loose upon the world."

"That happened at graduation." Deborah, the serious one, stared at her phone. "Will we have service on that mountain?"

Shea doubted it. "All I know is we've rented a large cabin overlooking the valley." The place had looked gorgeous online.

"I think it's going to storm most of the time." Rachel tended to look on the dark side of things.

"No, it won't." Emma shook her head. "I won't allow it to. This weekend is going to be perfect."

If the growing excitement in the van as they neared Misty Hollow was any indication, the weekend would be just as they all hoped. A time to reminisce, reconnect, and maybe relive a little of their college days when the ten of them had been inseparable. Since graduation, most of their contact took place online.

Shea leaned her head back and closed her eyes, content to listen as the others chattered about marriage and babies, neither of which she had anything to add to the conversation.

Misty Hollow's former sheriff, a man named Westbrook, had congratulated her on the fact no one had run against her. Why was that? No one knew her there from Adam—or Eve. She'd contacted Westbrook upon hearing of his retirement, sent in some letters of recommendation, and the next thing she knew, she wore a star on her chest.

If she were honest with herself, the whole situation left her apprehensive. Plus, a couple of the deputies had left when Westbrook retired, which meant Shea also had to find replacements. One more reason she needed to be at work and not on the top of a mountain.

"I can hear your brain from here," Becky said. "You aren't supposed to report to the office until Monday. Enjoy the next three days, okay?"

She cracked one eye open. "I'm trying."

"You always were the serious one." Becky patted

Shea's leg. "You really need to learn to relax."

"I was relaxing until you started talking." Shea grinned to take the sting out of her words.

Her friend giggled. "Maybe you'll find a man in Misty Hollow. One that can handle your moodiness."

"Ha, ha." Shea didn't have time for romance. Her career took up too much of her time, and that's the way she preferred her life to be. Men only complicated things.

"I'm going to stop here to get gas." Becky turned in front of a small, one-pump gas station. "We're headed up the mountain from here."

"I didn't see the town." Annie peered out the window.

"We're on the opposite side of Misty Mountain," Shea explained. "Going through the town would've added time to our drive." She shoved her door open. "I'll take care of the gas since you've driven the whole way."

"You don't have to do that, but thanks." Becky smiled.

Shea exited the van and filled the tank. She started to pay with her card but noticed the sign that said to pay inside. Great. She'd get caught up in a conversation with a bored employee.

The aroma of fried chicken and hot pizza greeted her as she pushed open the door. She pasted on a smile and approached the counter. "I'm here to pay for the gas."

The middle-aged man in denim overalls peered around her. "Where y'all headed?"

Shea slapped forty dollars on the counter. "We've rented a cabin on Eagle's Bluff."

His eyebrows rose. "Folks don't go up that way much. Haven't in a long time."

"Why not? The photos looked gorgeous."

"Oh, it's pretty enough." He rang up the gas and handed her the change.

Shea waited for him to say more. For several seconds, they stood and stared at each other before he finally spoke.

"You gals be careful up there."

"Wild animals?"

"Something like that." His gaze bore into hers.

Again, she expected him to say more. She almost identified herself as the new sheriff but decided against it. This weekend she was only Shea Callahan, not Sheriff Callahan.

"You gals come try out our pizza if you don't want to cook. You won't be sorry."

"Thanks." Shea flashed a smile and left the store. The back of her neck prickled, and she glanced back to see the man staring after her. She shuddered, remembering stories about the strangeness of mountain folk.

The man turned away first and said something to someone she couldn't see. Her law enforcement instinct left her feeling uneasy.

She slid back into the van. "Let's get out of here. Folks are strange."

Becky shot her a questioning look. "What is that smell?"

"Fried chicken and pizza."

"Oh, good. We know where to eat tonight. I'm sure no one feels like cooking after the long drive." She pulled from the station and continued up the mountain.

"I don't eat pizza," Emma said. "Too many carbs."

"Carbs don't count on girls' weekend," Rachel said from the back. "Everyone knows that."

Laughter erupted as the others agreed.

They arrived at a large A-frame cabin on the side of a bluff. A back deck hung over where the ground steeply sloped toward the cliff.

"It's beautiful. I have no idea why no one comes here." Shea glanced around the heavily wooded area. A creek babbled not far from the cabin.

"What do you mean no one comes here?" Tessa's eyes narrowed. "It's way more secluded than I thought. We haven't passed another house for miles. It's kind of spooky, and we're going to be here for almost a week."

Shea shrugged. "The man at the gas station seemed surprised we were coming here. He said no one comes here anymore." It couldn't be the price, because it had been ridiculously low for such a place. She'd thought they were getting a good deal when Becky sent her the link. Now she wasn't so sure. A shadow hovered over the beauty of the place. Even her friends had quieted. Whether from the same feeling that something wasn't quite right, or they simply were in awe of the scenery.

Shea hoped they wouldn't regret their decision to come. A bad weekend could go on forever

Read the rest here

www.cynthiahickey.com

Cynthia Hickey is a multi-published and best-selling author of cozy mysteries and romantic suspense. She has taught writing at many conferences and small writing retreats. She and her husband run the publishing press, Winged Publications. They live in Arizona and Arkansas, becoming snowbirds with three dogs. They have ten grandchildren who keep them busy and tell everyone they know that "Nana is a writer."

Connect with me on FaceBook
Twitter
Sign up for my newsletter and receive a free short story
www.cynthiahickey.com

Follow me on Amazon
And Bookbub
Shop my bookstore on shopify. For better price and autographed books. You can also subscribe to Mysterious Delivery, a mystery and suspense monthly book subscription with a book and several surprise goodies to pamper the reader.

Enjoy other books by Cynthia Hickey

Cowboys of Misty Hollow

Cowboy Jeopardy
Cowboy Peril
Cowboy Hazard
Cowgirl Blaze
Cowboy Uncertainty
Cowboy Christmas Crisis

Girls' Weekend Survival

Misty Hollow
Secrets of Misty Hollow
Deceptive Peace
Calm Surface
Lightning Never Strikes Twice
Lethal Inheritance
Bitter Isolation
Say I Don't
Christmas Stalker
Bridge to Safety
When Night Falls
A Place to Hide
Mountain Refuge

Stay in Misty Hollow for a while. Get the entire series here!

The Seven Deadly Sins series
Deadly Pride
Deadly Covet
Deadly Lust

Deadly Glutton
Deadly Envy
Deadly Sloth
Deadly Anger

The Tail Waggin' Mysteries
Cat-Eyed Witness
The Dog Who Found a Body
Troublesome Twosome
Four-Legged Suspect
Unwanted Christmas Guest
Wedding Day Cat Burglar

Brothers Steele
Sharp as Steele
Carved in Steele
Forged in Steele
Brothers Steele (All three in one)

The Brothers of Copper Pass
Wyatt's Warrant
Dirk's Defense
Stetson's Secret
Houston's Hope
Dallas's Dare
Seth's Sacrifice
Malcolm's Misunderstanding
The Brothers of Copper Pass Boxed Set

Time Travel

The Portal

Tiny House Mysteries
No Small Caper
Caper Goes Missing
Caper Finds a Clue
Caper's Dark Adventure
A Strange Game for Caper
Caper Steals Christmas
Caper Finds a Treasure
Tiny House Mysteries boxed set

Wife for Hire – Private Investigators
Saving Sarah
Lesson for Lacey
Mission for Meghan
Long Way for Lainie
Aimed at Amy
Wife for Hire (all five in one)

A Hollywood Murder
Killer Pose, book 1
Killer Snapshot, book 2
Shoot to Kill, book 3
Kodak Kill Shot, book 4
To Snap a Killer
Hollywood Murder Mysteries

Shady Acres Mysteries

Beware the Orchids, book 1
Path to Nowhere
Poison Foliage
Poinsettia Madness
Deadly Greenhouse Gases
Vine Entrapment
Shady Acres Boxed Set

CLEAN BUT GRITTY Romantic Suspense

Highland Springs

Murder Live
Say Bye to Mommy
To Breathe Again
Highland Springs Murders (all 3 in one)

Colors of Evil Series

Shades of Crimson
Coral Shadows

The Pretty Must Die Series

Ripped in Red, book 1
Pierced in Pink, book 2
Wounded in White, book 3
Worthy, The Complete Story

Lisa Paxton Mystery Series

Eenie Meenie Miny Mo
Jack Be Nimble
Hickory Dickory Dock
Boxed Set

Hearts of Courage
A Heart of Valor
The Game
Suspicious Minds
After the Storm
Local Betrayal
Hearts of Courage Boxed Set

Overcoming Evil series
Mistaken Assassin
Captured Innocence
Mountain of Fear
Exposure at Sea
A Secret to Die for
Collision Course
Romantic Suspense of 5 books in 1

INSPIRATIONAL

Nosy Neighbor Series
Anything For A Mystery, Book 1
A Killer Plot, Book 2
Skin Care Can Be Murder, Book 3

Death By Baking, Book 4
Jogging Is Bad For Your Health, Book 5
Poison Bubbles, Book 6
A Good Party Can Kill You, Book 7
Nosy Neighbor collection

Christmas with Stormi Nelson

The Summer Meadows Series
Fudge-Laced Felonies, Book 1
Candy-Coated Secrets, Book 2
Chocolate-Covered Crime, Book 3
Maui Macadamia Madness, Book 4
All four novels in one collection

The River Valley Mystery Series
Deadly Neighbors, Book 1
Advance Notice, Book 2
The Librarian's Last Chapter, Book 3
All three novels in one collection

Historical cozy
Hazel's Quest

Historical Romances
Runaway Sue
Taming the Sheriff
Sweet Apple Blossom

A Doctor's Agreement
A Lady Maid's Honor
A Touch of Sugar
Love Over Par
Heart of the Emerald
A Sketch of Gold
Her Lonely Heart

Finding Love the Harvey Girl Way
Cooking With Love
Guiding With Love
Serving With Love
Warring With Love
All 4 in 1

Finding Love in Disaster
The Rancher's Dilemma
The Teacher's Rescue
The Soldier's Redemption

Woman of courage Series

A Love For Delicious
Ruth's Redemption
Charity's Gold Rush
Mountain Redemption
They Call Her Mrs. Sheriff
Woman of Courage series

Short Story Westerns
Flowers of the Desert

Contemporary

Romance in Paradise
Maui Magic
Sunset Kisses
Deep Sea Love
3 in 1

Finding a Way Home
Service of Love
Hillbilly Cinderella
Unraveling Love
I'd Rather Kiss My Horse

Christmas
Dear Jillian
Romancing the Fabulous Cooper Brothers
Handcarved Christmas
The Payback Bride
Curtain Calls and Christmas Wishes
Christmas Gold
A Christmas Stamp
Snowflake Kisses
Merry's Secret Santa
A Christmas Deception

The Red Hat's Club (Contemporary novellas)

<u>Finally</u>
<u>Suddenly</u>
<u>Surprisingly</u>
<u>The</u> Red Hat's Club 3 – in 1

<u>Short Story</u>

<u>One Hour (A short story thriller)</u>
<u>Whisper Sweet Nothings (a Valentine short romance)</u>